RAINBOW RIDER

Bill Dawson is a man seeking the pot of gold at the rainbow's end. He drifts into a small cow town, only to buy himself a packet of trouble with the Big S retainers. Soon he is working for the Trents, and enraptured by the lovely Lila. Ultimately, he finds himself on the side of the small-time farmers on Government land who are being crowded out by the Big S . . .

D. B. NEWTON

RAINBOW RIDER

Complete and Unabridged

LINFORD
Leicester

First published in the United States by Ace Books
First published in the United Kingdom by
Macdonald & Co.

First Linford Edition
published 2021
by arrangement with
Golden West Literary Agency

*A catalogue record for this book is available
from the British Library.*

ISBN 978–1–78541–959–1

Published by
Ulverscroft Limited
Anstey, Leicestershire

Printed and bound in Great Britain by
TJ Books Ltd., Padstow, Cornwall

This book is printed on acid-free paper

1

There seemed nothing out of the way about this Bill Dawson, the day he came across the passes into Renner Valley. A chilled soaked figure, shouldering deep inside a bulky rubber poncho with head bowed to the needling of the rain — he looked like any fiddle-footed grubline rider. As a matter of fact, the pockets of Bill Dawson's jeans were nearly empty, and maybe a half dozen smokes remained in his limp Bull Durham bag. But his grey eyes, behind lashes finely beaded with the rain, showed a fiddle-foot's unyielding confidence in the rainbow that must lie somewhere just ahead.

Actually, his present discomfort was small enough after bucking the deep-drifted snow that clogged the passes. By contrast, these lower hills held welcome springtime greenness; many rivulets of melt-water, chocolate-coloured and noisy, kept pace with a rider as he dropped down the timbered slants. And where the steep land first grew level enough for a town to cling to it, he found Renner City.

For all it was a county seat, and had a big red court house, this place looked bleak enough. Some years back the collapse of a promising silver boom had left it stranded, with the nearest railroad fifty miles away; in consequence, every pound of supplies the town consumed must be hauled in by wagon freight, over a long and dangerous trail. Drifting into the head of the single thoroughfare, now, his bay gelding's irons slipping and sucking deep into mire, Bill Dawson saw a heavy-duty Pittsburgh rig and string team standing before a mercantile's loading platform; a man in a red mackinaw was busily emptying the big wagon of crates and boxes.

He paused a moment, to give the outfit an appraising glance. He'd handled a jerkine himself, on occasion — between other jobs as irrigation ditch rider, sawmill chainsetter, surveyor's rodman, or hop picker. Just name it: one time or another, Bill Dawson had probably done it. Mostly however, he'd punched cattle when such work was to be had. And when he had shoved warm food under his belt he meant to inquire the trail to this Big S spread, down-valley, where he understood someone named Steve Slate was hiring new men — lots of men . . .

Nearly broke though he was, he first of all hunted up a public livery where he spent part of his remaining cash on a bait of oats for the weary gelding; then, on foot, he back tracked to a lunch counter that he'd spotted. It was a relief to be quit of the storm. He dragged off his limp hat, shook the moisture from it and hung it up. The poncho came over his head with a single jerk at the rubbery material, and he dumped this in a wet, stiff heap on the floor.

Without it, he shaped up as a well-built man, neither short nor tall, and with hips fined down by much time in the saddle. His Levis were stuffed into high, flatheeled boots; his leather jacket partly concealed a brush-scarred holster and shell belt strapped to a narrow waist. The Bisley .45 was rubber-butted; efficient, without any fanciness — like everything else about Bill Dawson.

'Came over the hills,' he told the man behind the counter, after he'd named his order, 'Some joker said the passes were open. Well, they certainly are now — I opened them! Looking for a man named Slater. Can you tell me how I find his ranch?'

The man in the grease-spotted apron gave him a glum look. 'Big S don't take no findin',' he grunted. 'Just foller the road down into the valley. You couldn't miss it.'

'Good-sized outfit, huh? Reckon they could use a lot of hands.'

The man shrugged. 'That would depend.'

'On what?'

'You better ask Steve Slater.'

Bill Dawson didn't press him, but went to work on the overdone beefsteak and the china cup of black coffee. The cook retired to the rear of the shack to make a clatter with dirty pans and dishes, cleaning up.

4

An occasional gust of wind flung sleety rain to batter the plate glass of the eat shack window, and fall away. Dawson gazed out into the muddy street as he ate, watching the few people who passed from time to time.

Then, suddenly, a cavalcade of half a dozen riders came drumming through the slop, held by it to a sort of slow-motion gallop, the irons of their horses splashing muddy water high. Dawson looked for brands, saw the sprawling Big S burn figured on a couple of the mounts. It occurred to him that the blocky, solid shape in the saddle of the forward bronc might even be Steve Slater himself; but before he could call the cook's attention to him the rider and his companions had gone from sight beyond the reach of the window.

Not wanting to miss a possible chance at the Big S boss, Bill Dawson quickly bolted the rest of his meal, draining off the coffee cup standing. Digging down, he rang his last silver dollar on the lunch counter in payment, then quickly snagged hat and poncho as he made for the door.

He dragged on the hat, merely bundled the bulky rain cape under one arm. The riders had vanished but a glance showed him their horses, warm hides steaming, at a whiskey mill tie-rack farther along the street. As he started in that direction, the sodden planks of the boardwalk thudded dully underfoot.

The saloon's winter doors were still up. Within he found an atmosphere that reeked of wet wool, horse sweat, and beer, and such a gloom from the storm outside that a couple of kerosene lamps above the bar had already been lighted. The half dozen men who belonged to the horses were lined along the mahogany with liquor glasses in front of them.

Bill Dawson moved over to the forward end of the counter where it angled off square against the side wall. He shook his head at the bartender, since he had not money enough left for a drink, and set himself to waiting patiently for a chance to approach the man he'd pegged as the owner of the Big S brand.

It was Slater, right enough — one of the others called him by that name. He was a big man, as big as he'd looked in the saddle, and somewhere over forty. He must have been remarkably handsome once, but had let soft living get in its work; had let it blur the clean lines of well-cut features, and put an unneeded weight of flesh upon a solid frame. Yet from his manner of dressing, and the very way he carried himself, it was evident that vanity still formed as dominant a part in his makeup as it ever had.

The men with him looked like ordinary saddle pounders; their talk was local range gossip, containing little of interest to a stranger. Once or twice Dawson heard the name 'McHail' spoken, along with angry references to 'those damn' sodbusters down-valley.' Nowadays, with farmers from the middle frontier pressing westward in a steady tide upon the cowman's domain, one was apt to hear such talk in any saloon, anywhere across the cattle country . . .

Presently the glass doors rattled, and someone entered in a gust of chilly dampness. Glancing around, Bill Dawson wondered where he had seen the lean figure in the bright red mackinaw; the windwhipped, lantern-jawed face. Then, of course, he remembered. A little while ago he had watched this man unloading a six-team freight rig, at the mercantile up the street.

The newcomer hesitated a moment as the combined stares of the Big S riders swung towards him. It seemed to Dawson that he looked almost frightened. But afterwards his face settled into stubborn defiance and he came ahead, passing up the cattlemen and seeking a place by himself farther along the counter. Putting his lean belly to the edge of it, he muttered something and was digging for change as the bartender turned to fetch him an unopened pint bottle.

Steve Slater had watched this purchase, his handsome face slowly twisting into a sneering grin. 'Look at this, boys!' he remarked, suddenly. 'Here's Tag

Klebold, celebrating! Could it be some-body's actually give him a consignment?'

If this was a joke, it hardly seemed to rate the chorus of hilarity it got from the Big S men. Slater joined them in laughing at his own wit, his head thrown back, his too-heavy body shaking gleefully. And the gibe went home.

Dawson saw Klebold's face go pale, saw the raw-knuckled hands tighten on the edge of the bar. The man was staring down at his hands, not glancing to right or left. He looked as though he were hoping to be able to weather this through and that nothing would come of it.

But Slater was in a mood for baiting. He drained off his glass, slapped it down on the sticky bar. 'How about that, Tag?' he prodded. 'You still hangin' on? How long you figure to cheat the glue factory with them hatracks you call freight teams?'

Klebold said tensely, still looking at the bar top, 'Don't ride me, Slater!'

'Why, I ain't riding you. Come to

think of it, maybe I'd even like to talk business!'

Grinning broadly, the big man circled his crew and moved ponderously towards the freighter, whom he outsized by half a head and the good part of a hundred pounds. He leaned a hip against the wood, and dragged out a choked cowhide wallet.

'Seems to me I'd listen, too, if I was you,' he went on, fumbling with the bills. 'Because it ain't likely you'll ever get another offer as good as this one . . . I'm gonna buy you out, Tag. All your equity — that miserable cavvy of livestock, and both them rigs you keep strung together witt balin' wire. I'll even allow real generous for good will. Look!'

He fished out a greenback and thrust it under Tag Klebold's nose. Bill Dawson saw a picture of Lincoln on the bill. Five dollars.

Amid another burst of laughter Klebold jerked his head away, slapping at the huge paw shoved into his face. The bill slipped from Slater's fingers, fluttered to the sawdust scattered floor.

'Damn you!' the scrawny freighter cried hoarsely. 'Leave me alone! What chance have I got, with you backing the Trents to grab every dollar of business between here and railhead? I'm in the same boat as those poor farmers, that are trying to hold their own against Big S . . .'

Steve Slater had lost all his humour, his dark face gone suddenly dangerous. 'All right, you've talked enough!' he said, warningly. 'Now, shut your mouth — or I might shut it for you.'

'You'll have to kill me, then,' shouted Klebold. 'That's the only way you'll ever stop me saying what I think of a filthy, crooked — '

Then he was making a wild lunge backward; but Slater moved too fast for him. Slater's slabby hand dropped upon his shoulder, and Klebold squirmed with pain under the bite of its grip. He shrilled, 'Lemme go!' He made a fumbling movement at the pocket of his mackinaw, where there was likely a gun.

That was a mistake. Bellowing rage, Steve Slater swung his other fist. It

11

slammed against the bony face and Tag Klebold went staggering sideways, driven nearly off his feet. Bill Dawson winced involuntarily as he heard the sickening, meaty smack of bruising knuckles. He saw Klebold stumble into the man next to Slater; saw that one grab him, whirl him around and deliver a blow of his own, in turn. And then Tag Klebold was going down the line of Big S riders, caroming from one man to the next, while their tongues cursed him and their fists gave him a solid working over.

Klebold's bony face blossomed red with spurting blood. There was no chance to get a guard up, to check the rain of blows or lash back at his tormentors. His punishment lasted only a matter of seconds; then with a final wallop he was sent spinning to the sawdust and lay there as though stunned.

Someone shouted, 'Go on! Give him the boot!'

The puncher at the end of the line moved willingly enough to do it, his lips drawn back in a grimace of savage pleasure. With one hand on the bar to balance himself he lifted a heavy cowhide, obviously meaning to drive its blunt toe into the body of the fallen man.

That was when Bill Dawson knew he would have to get into this.

He didn't want to; he had ridden a long way on the hope of finding a job with Big S, and he hated to throw away his chance for nothing. But ribs would crack and cave if that boot landed; and just as the kick started, his hand shot impulsively across the angle of the bar, grabbing the puncher's braced wrist and jerking sharply.

Slater's man was hurled off balance by the force of his own movement. Pivoting, he struck the bar's edge; the wind gusted out of him. He buckled, slid helpless to his knees. And at the same moment, the shouting of the Big S men quit off — exactly as though a knife blade had gone slicing through it.

A moment's stunned quiet ended abruptly, then, as the man Dawson had upset came clawing his way up the face of the bar, sobbing for wind. 'Who done that?' he cried hoarsely. 'Lemme lay my fists on him!'

He was fighting the skirt of his hung-open slicker, trying to free the holstered gun beneath. It was not a time for diplomacy; given no other choice, Dawson hastily jerked his own weapon out and he rapped its barrel sharply on the mahogany.

'Leave the gun alone, fellow,' he ordered. 'Let's not make something big out of a little thing!'

'Why, you — !' Wisely, the man checked himself. Bill Dawson, however, didn't fail to recognize the menace in the angry eyes he saw before him.

He said, 'Maybe you'd all better put your hands on the wood, where I can see them. Everybody, I mean!'

Slowly, with the most evident reluctance, six pairs of hands edged up into sight and came to rest on top of the bar. Then Steve Slater spoke, and his words held the tightness of suppressed rage.

14

'What sort of a damn fool are you? Put away that gun, you hear me?'

'No! Don't do it — don't give 'em an inch!' Tag Klebold, down in the sawdust, had rolled to hands and knees now and he lifted a blood-smeared face, to stare wildly at the line-up of prisoners. 'They're treacherous! You don't want to get careless, mister — not at this stage of the game!'

Dawson had it figured the same way; the barrel of his gun stayed just as it was, slanted across the angle of the bar's end. 'Klebold,' he suggested, 'maybe you better leave, while I've got the hobbles on them. They should calm down some, once you're gone.'

'Maybe so . . . Well — thanks, mister! Thanks a lot!'

'That's O.K.,' said Dawson. 'Forget it.'

Klebold got shakily to his feet. He smeared a sleeve across his battered face. 'But don't think, Slater,' he added, hotly, 'that you're gonna keep on pushing people around, forever. One of these times

15

you'll go just too far. You, and that Jabez Trent — '

Bill Dawson cut him off impatiently. 'Will you get out? That's the kind of talk started the trouble, in the first place . . . '

The man turned abruptly on his heel, clomped away. For a moment after the door slammed behind him and the loose pane in it rattled to silence, there was no sound in the room but for the harsh breathing of angry men, and the ticking of a banjo clock above the bar.

Dawson took air into his own cramped lungs. 'Look,' he ventured. 'If you fellows are ready to drop this, I know I am. I suppose I shouldn't have barged in on some thing that was none of my business.' He laid the Bisley .45 down on the bartop in front of him, put his empty hands on either side of it. 'Quits, huh?'

'I ain't so sure.' Steve Slater's eyes were buried in a scowl of simmering anger. 'Just who are you, anyway? And what do you want?'

Dawson told his name, which of course meant nothing to the big man. 'This is gonna sound kind of silly,' he finished, 'but I was meaning to brace you for a job — '

'You were *what*?' roared Slater. 'Why, you just set foot on Big S graze and watch me, personally, boot you clean into Wyoming!'

The stranger nodded, resignedly. 'I was afraid it would be like that,' he admitted; adding, with a fiddle-foot's pride, 'Still, after what I've seen, maybe I wouldn't really be crazy about riding for such an outfit.' To the bartender he said, 'I think Klebold paid you for that bottle. Just scoot it along to me and I'll see that he gets it . . . Thanks.'

A flip of the barman's wrist sent the pint of whiskey sliding down the mahogany, past the six pairs of hands. Bill Dawson scooped it up and then palmed the Bisley, his wet poncho under one elbow. He still hesitated, though, looking at that line of glaring faces. 'No hard feelings, gents?' he suggested, anxiously.

'Why, when I get my hands on you — ' began the man he had winded; but Steve

Slater cut this outburst short.

'Let it go!' he ordered, sourly. 'Go on, Dawson — or whatever your name is. Beat it! Take Klebold his liquor. Also, I've got a message for him, while you're at it. Tell the sneakin' coyote I'm through fooling with him. I don't want his ratty freight teams crossing my range, and I've already given orders to shoot any that try it. You got that straight?'

The other nodded, bleakly. 'I reckon.'

'All right — tell him!' Slater jerked his big head at the door. 'Start walkin', while we're still of a mood to let you . . . '

2

Once through the door, Bill Dawson moved quickly to place his back against the drab, rain-soaked clapboards of the saloon facing and wait like that a moment, one hand clutching the butt of the six-gun he'd returned to its holster. His shoulder muscles, he found, were knotted and aching; it had taken real nerve to turn his back on those dangerous men, and to cross the long expanse of spur-scarred floor, feeling their eyes bore into him at every step. Under his chill, wet clothes, he was sweating freely.

But though hc waited, nothing happened. He could hear faintly the buzz of talk resuming inside the building, but no one started after him. Still, there was little use tempting fate. Now that he had queered himself for the job he'd come here hoping to find, the wisest thing to do would be to get his bay gelding from the stable, at once, and leave.

First, though, he still had Tag Klebold's pint, and Klebold's freight wagon and string stood a few doors up the hill, in front of the mercantile. Bill Dawson shifted the bulky bundle of wet poncho under his elbow and started that way, through the needling rain that seemed to be easing off a little now. There was a dazzle-streak across the grey cloud ceiling, that might mean it would be clearing after a bit.

Approaching the rig, he could see nothing of the freighter but thought he heard movement within the canvas-topped wagon box. He called Klebold's name; there was no answer for a moment, and then the man shot a scared look around the edge of the forward bow. 'Oh — it's you!' He showed plain relief.

Bill Dawson held up the bottle. 'Something you forgot. Catch!'

He tossed it and Klebold took it out of the air. 'Thanks!' he grunted, still eyeing the man on the soggy boardwalk. He had a towel in his hand, with which he'd been dabbing at the cuts on his face. 'Say, fellow,' he croaked in a hoarse voice. 'You better git!'

'Why, I'd say the same to you,' remarked Bill Dawson, drily.

'Never mind — I'm gittin'!' Klebold flung his towel into the wagon, came climbing out across the seatback to settle into his place.

'There was a message that Slater asked me to pass on to you,' said Dawson. He repeated the warning, word for word. Klebold's bony face went hard as he listened.

'Maybe he thinks I'm scared of him!' the freighter grunted harshly.

Bill Dawson could have said that, in the face of the evidence, it very possibly might be. Instead, he answered merely, 'I just told you what he told me . . . Well, take it easy.'

'I'm headin' south,' Klebold suggested. 'Give you a lift?'

The other shook his head. 'I got a bronc at the livery.' Still, he lingered a moment in the rain, watching Klebold's preparations to depart.

21

It was a jerkline team the man had hitched to his freight rig, the horses managed by a single string run along to the bridle of the near leader, its other end anchored to the big brake handle. Such a team could be worked either from the high seat, or from a saddle on the near wheeler's back.

One jerk, two jerks on the line, and the canny lead animal got its signal and pulled or pushed its mate in the desired direction, the rest of the horses leaping expertly from side to side of the long centre chain in executing sharp corners. It took a good man to train or handle a jerkline team; some impulse made Dawson ask suddenly, 'Wouldn't be any chance of a job, would there?'

Klebold, one hand on the brake lever, slanted a look at him. 'With me? You know anything about this kind of outfit?'

'Why, I've skinned a few mules. Horses, too. Not much I haven't tackled, one time or another.'

'I'd say you look more like a cow-puncher.'

'Maybe so. But it don't look like I'm apt to get a chance to punch any, around here — not if Steve Slater has anything to say about it. Meanwhile, I need cash, I got to eat; and there's nothing much in my jeans but me.'

The freighter hesitated. 'Well, I guess it's my fault your goose got cooked with Slater. And it's a fact I'm gonna be needing a driver before too long, the way business is looking . . . Well, if you're not afraid of trouble with Big S, climb in. We'll pick up your bronc at the stable, and then talk things over as we go.'

Not much later, with Bill's gelding following on a whale line and his stock saddle thrown in the empty wagon, they were rattling away from that misnamed Renner City and following an excruciating horror of rutted road, that looped southward into the big funnel that was the valley.

High foothills broke against the rims at either hand; westward, the head of Renner Peak was lost in shifting cloud wrack. The overcast was dissolving now, however, and shafts of watery sunlight filtered through to ease a little the chill of the air, and touch with sudden gleams of eye-punishing brightness this range that was greening up beautifully under the spring rains.

'I couldn't pay you a hell of a lot to begin with,' Tag Klebold was saying, above the jounce and thunder of the empty rig. 'Not much better than swamper's wages, Slater ain't really far wrong about the value of my business what it's been, up to now, anyway. I'm hardly more'n a damn shotgun freighter, pickin' up a nickel's worth of trade here and there, where I can. Still, I'm buckin' a tough set up.'

'You mean this Jabez Trent?'

'The same!' Klebold spat across the turning wheel. 'Old man Trent — with Slater's money backin' him — he's got his hooks into every pound of freight that's moved west of the railhead at Fair Play, But my toe is in the door now, and I'll bust that monopoly. Just as Tom McHail and the farmers are going to

24

kick Slater clean out of South Renner, if he don't let 'em alone . . . Here, take a look at this.'

He fumbled out a crumpled fold of paper and handed it over, a leer of triumph on his battered face. The paper was a contract, dated that day, between Klebold and the syndicate manager of one of the two silver mines still producing ore back in the lower hills. It gave Tag Klebold exclusive commission in the future to transport all supplies to the mine from railhead, and carry the ore to the smelter. The agreed rate was high enough to draw a low whistle from the drifter.

'Not bad, huh?' the freighter exulted, returning the paper to his pocket, 'That's the opening wedge, fellow! Until today, all I've had was some small-time stuff that the Trents didn't happen to want-like this here mercantile in Renner, which means hauling half a load up and going back empty, so you don't more'n break even. But now - - ' He slapped the pocket in high enthusiasm. 'I'll have to put more wagons on the road, right away. And if you can handle a team, there could be plenty of work in it for you.'

'Do I understand you took this account out from under Jabez Trent's nose? That must have needed some doing!'

'Couldn't have been easier. Naturally, though,' Klebold added, lowering his voice a little, 'a man's got to know how to play all the angles. Like this joker at the mine — '

He leaned closer, with a furtive look around — almost as though he were afraid of being overheard. But plainly this matter was something he wanted badly to brag about, even if to a total stranger.

'You savvy the situation: a Company man, bein' paid a salary too stinkin' low for any self-respecting gent to put up with, while the syndicate bosses make a cleaning. Well, naturally, he was ripe for the right kind of a deal. And at the same time, I'm naturally glad to take the account for a lot lower figure than what's writ down there in ink on the contract.

We're both making a profit. See what I mean?'

'I think so.' Bill Dawson saw, and something chilled over between him and the other man on the seat. 'The old kickback.'

'What else?' A gusty wheeze of laughter, and Klebold's bony elbow jabbing his ribs, gave emphasis to this cleverness. But then, sensing a certain lack of response in the other, Klebold went suddenly quiet, turning on Dawson a narrow and suspicious look. 'Or — maybe you don't approve?'

Dawson shrugged briefly. 'I didn't say so.'

'Well, the hell with you!' Klebold was growing angry. 'I say a man's got to fight with the same weapons as his enemies. And lemme tell you this: should you get any ideas of repeatin' what you just learned, there ain't a word of it you could prove!

'So if you don't like my way of doin' business, then take your bronc and your saddle, for all I care, and git the hell away from me! D'you hear? Git!'

But Bill Dawson stayed where he was, scowling stubbornly at the bobbing rumps of the horses strung out ahead. For just an instant he found himself remembering what Steve Slater had called this man beside him: *a sneakin' coyote!* Well — could be. But then, after all, what was Slater?

And for that matter, what was Bill Dawson but a drifter down to the lining of his pockets, and in no position to be choosy about the man he worked for?

So what he said was, 'I hire for wages. I try to do a job, and I trust my boss to know what he's up to.'

Tag Klebold was one given to sudden changes of mood. His sourness instantly dissolving, he laughed again and gave the other a clap on the shoulder. 'Why, now, that's more like it! You just wait'll you see some of the dirty work that goes on around here. You'll likely agree, then, there's only one way a man can fight it — with more of the same!'

He added, turning abruptly business-like, 'But I don't even know if you can really handle a string team or not. Let's go to work and have a look at what you can do with this one.'

It was an easy, looping course the road took, across downward-sweeping bunch grass range. Tag Klebold seemed well enough satisfied as Bill Dawson took over the check-line and the long, sinuous whip which was a teamster's badge of office.

This was truly a ratty outfit, the horses gaunted and listless — culls and cast-offs, probably, from more prosperous freight lines, picked up cheap by Tag Klebold when their former owners discarded them as too old and useless for anything but the glue factory. They knew their work, however, and there was not enough spirit left in any of them to make them hard to handle.

Klebold left the new man to manage the teams while he fetched out the pint bottle he'd bought in town and broke it open, ran the liquor into him. He offered the other a pull, but Bill Dawson declined it; they rolled on down the deep trough of the valley, making good time with an empty wagon.

The sun came through and at once the wet earth began to steam in wavering wisps that walked across the greening slopes and hollows. It looked like good range country. The cattle they saw spotting the rises seemed well fleshed out, for so early in season. Once they passed quite near to where Big S hands were working a jag of whiteface cows and calves; there was the increase to be marked and branded, and then the beef would be moved up into the hills as spring advanced and summer range opened up, back under the flanks of Renner Peak.

A busy time of year, and saddle work that Bill Dawson liked. Aud yet here he was, tooling a creaking wagon and scrawny jerkline team, while the slovenly, lantern-jawed scarecrow who was his new employer sprawled on the seat beside him, and worried his whiskey bottle. Well, so it went. If he found he couldn't stomach this job he could always throw it over after drawing down a few weeks' pay, and with that in his jeans start riding on. There were other ranges, and other outfits would be hiring . . .

They arrived presently at the place where a ground spring came brawling down a rocky foothill spur, hard by a wide loop of the trail that brought them in close to the timber. The horses, as though following familiar routine, pulled off onto a flat and halted, and Klebold said, 'I generally water them here — handiest point in the north valley. You take care of them, will you? Seems like the squeak in that off hind wheel has a funny new pitch to it. I better check and see it ain't ready to fall off.'

He swung his gaunt frame down the high wheel. Bill set the brake, shoved his whip into the socket and vaulted down. With the creaking and jolt of the wagon stilled, as well as the pound of hoofs and the rattle of harness, he found a great quietness in the day. A breeze swayed the bunch grass softly; stunted pine on a near slope murmured above the voice of the spring, and somewhere a lark whistled in the meadow. After the cold misery of crossing snow-packed hills and shivering under drizzling rain, this steaming sunlight had an expansive power. Bill Dawson was feeling prime as he set to work unhitching the teams, by pairs, and moving them down to the water.

Tag Klebold had a rock and was pounding the offending wheel with it, trying to settle it on the thimble; but as Dawson returned with the second pair of horses this sound all at once ceased and Tag Klebold grunted a warning: 'Look sharp, boy!' At the same instant, Dawson first caught the drum of riders coming in at a good pace.

Quickly he snapped the pair onto the chain and then stepped around the wagon for a look. There were three of them, heading straight towards the freight outfit. 'Big S men,' muttered Klebold, from under a shading palm. 'That's Virg Noonan in the middle — range boss for

Slater. He can make trouble.'

'Will he know what happened in town?' Dawson asked anxiously.

'Not likely he's had time to hear . . . '

The rhythm of the cantering horses beat against them. Then the riders had pulled to a plunging, stiff-legged halt. The leader threw his voice at the pair upon the ground: 'You got two minutes to get that rig to rolling!'

It began to look as though this Big S outfit ran to large men. Virg Noonan shaped up big in the saddle; maybe he had not quite the heft of Steve Slater himself, but on the other hand his poundage was all good meat, with none of Slater's excess weight around the belly. His face, like his body, was blunt and wide. His mouth was wide, too, and there was a gold tooth in the front of it.

'We'll roll when we've done!' the gaunt freighter retorted. 'We ain't stepping on *your* corns, that I know of!' Virg Noonan gave him an insolent appraisal, out of heavily lidded eyes. He had a braided riding quirt slung from one gauntleted wrist and he swung this by its thong, idly. 'A new ruling, Tag. Them hayburners of yours eat up too much grass. We want you to keep them off Big S.'

Angry colour began to show in Klebold's neck and prominent ears. 'It's a public road that runs through here. I got business on it. You can't order me off.'

'But I *can* tell you to keep moving, and not let these boneracks get out of the ruts and onto our graze. Slater's instructions are to shoot 'em if they do.'

'This is the first I've heard of it! 'said Tag Klebold — which, as it happened, was not exactly true.

The range boss shrugged, indifferently. 'You're hearin' it now. This time, you can take the critters and git. But this time don't mean next time! Then, we start shooting!'

'I always water here. My teams can't manage the haul clear up to North Renner without a blow at least once on the trip.'

'If they was more than half alive they

could,' Noonan retorted with heavy humour. 'Hell, you can haul grain for 'em, can't you? Feed 'em out of nose-bags. Waterin' 'em don't cost us nothing; but henceforth, any nag that so much as lays a tooth to a blade of Big S grass gets turned into soap stock, pronto!' He straightened in the saddle, his mouth and tone went hard. 'Now, beat it!'

The danger was there, sharp and distinct, but Tag Klebold had shown that he possessed a capacity for stubbornness against reckless odds. It wasn't wisdom to go on arguing in the teeth of that ultimatum. Still, he did it. 'My man here ain't finished watering 'em yet.'

'Oh, yes he has!' For the first time Noonan gave the stranger a flick of attention; it was only a sidelong glance, and a jerk of Noonan's solid head towards the high seat of the wagon. 'Crawl up there — both of you. And clear out, while I'm settin' here to see that you do!'

Well, that was it — the direct order, the challenge, the threat. Virg Noonan meant business. He had men with him, and they all three wore guns. Bill Dawson had a gun, too; but Tag Klebold's weapon was in a pocket of his mackinaw, and he had shed that garment with the coming of warming sunlight — it was up in the wagon, completely out of reach. So this was no time to offer an argument.

Nevertheless Bill Dawson made no move to obey the instructions Noonan had laid on him. Instead he dragged a slow breath, turned to look at Tag Klebold.

'You're the one pays my wages,' he said gruffly. 'What's your orders?'

Fists clenched, jaw trembling, Klebold glared at the Big S foreman and hurled defiant answer. 'Them wheelers ain't drunk yet. Unhook 'em, boy, and lead 'em to the spring!'

'Right!' And Dawson turned, deliberately, and reached for the harness of the wheel team.

Next instant he heard the snort of Noonan's roan under the spurs, felt the jar of the earth as its iron-shod hoofs bit in. He whirled quickly. The horse was lunging straight upon him, the man in its saddle seemingly bent on riding him down. Rolling eyeballs, flaring nostrils and mane streaming above sleek red hide hung between him and the sky. For a breathless moment Bill's footing slipped. He threw out a hand in an attempt to grab the roan's bridle, force it off him.

Then, too late, he saw Virg Noonan's real aim — saw the quirt descending. He had no chance to duck. The braided thongs struck, and a good eight inches of the weighted stock as well. He took the blow partly on cheek and ear, mostly on the side of the neck; then the quirt rose and fell again, twice more, whipping him. He stumbled in his effort to escape it, and sprawled flat.

During a long, humiliating minute he could only lie there, numb with pain and with a ringing in his head caused by those punishing blows across the ear. Through it he heard dimly the angry shouting of voices. Then fury brought him scrambling up to his feet, hunting out his attacker while he fumbled for the handle of his Bisley .45. But he didn't touch it.

For a gunsear clicked, and the warning sound held him. One of the men with Noonan had slipped his weapon and was holding it as a threat against Bill Dawson; he was a little pale as he looked to his boss for a further cue, but the gun was steady enough in his hand and Bill caught himself, having sense enough to respect its danger.

Yonder, Virg Noonan had pulled his roan back now. Still utterly unruffled, and without bothering to draw a gun, he was placing his final ultimatum in front of a thoroughly scared Tag Klebold.

'If you want some of what I gave your swamper, just stick around. Otherwise, get up on the box and start this outfit moving!'

But now Bill Dawson, half choking, had found his voice and he hurled a furious challenge. 'Climb off that bronc, damn you! Tell your man to put his gun away, or I'll knock that gold tooth clean through the back of your neck. You can wear it for a collar stud on Sundays!'

Noonan gave him a slow, contemptuous stare. 'Shut up,' he grunted, heavily.

Hands curled into fists, the other shouted, 'I'm not used to being horse-whipped!'

'No?' Virg Noonan had straightened suddenly; his eye was hard, now, and now a gun slid into his fingers. 'One more word, and I'll pistol whip you!' He looked over at Klebold, utterly dismissing the man he had struck down. 'The orders stand. Have these nags moving inside two minutes or I'm apt to change my mind and start shootin' 'em!'

'No! Don't do it!' Thoroughly cowed, now, and lacking all defiance, Klebold was falling over himself in his frantic haste to scramble up the wheel to the seat. He had a boot poised to kick off the brake as he rolled a scared eye at his hired man, who still stood glaring at the Big S range boss. 'Hurry up!' he begged. 'Leave well enough alone and let's get out of here!'

Bill Dawson surfaced like a diver,

breaking through his anger with a shake of the head as though to clear it. His hat lay on the ground in front of him; he leaned and got it, straightened, running the back of a fist across the side of his head and looked at the slight smear of blood he found there. Damaged pride was an angry tumult within him.

But with a pair of guns pointed at him, there was no outlet for this; he had to swallow his rage, dragging on the hat with a vicious tug at its rain-soggy brim. He laid one final glance upon Virg Noonan, that was both a challenge and a silent promise that this incident was not closed according to his reckoning. Then, turning his back on the Big S man's mocking stare, he heeled about and walked over to the wagon, as Klebold straightened out his whip with a crack above the steaming backs of the horses.

Dawson stepped onto a spoke of the turning front wheel and rode it up, swinging easily to the seat and settling himself there beside the freighter. He leaned then for a final scowling look back at the three horsemen, sitting saddle motionlessly to watch them roll away. He stayed like that until the jolting rig was on the trail again; and when he squared around, his face was white from withheld emotion.

'He may be sorry for that some day!' he muttered, dangerously.

Tag Klebold slid him a sideways look, and shrugged bony shoulders. 'Forget it!' he muttered. 'Here.' Fishing around on the seat behind him, he came up with the half-empty pint bottle. 'Take a drag of this to cool you off.'

The other only shook his head impatiently, waving the bottle away; so Klebold upended the pint to his own lips and lowered its contents another inch. His hand was shaking with the aftermath of fear as he palmed the cork home, stowed the liquor away into a pocket.

'I know how you feel,' he grunted heavily. 'Lord knows I been kicked around enough by that outfit, and by the Trents, to appreciate it. But, hell! you can't fight 'em — not with fists or guns. If we'd tried it, back there, we'd have ended up with our horses shot and the wagon burned down to the tyre-irons; maybe even worse.

'No,' he decided, 'you got to get around 'em in other ways. Ways like this here.' And he tapped the pocket where a fold of paper crackled.

Bill Dawson didn't bother to answer. He rode hunched forward, arms on knees and hands dangling to the jostle of the rig, and he stared at the rumps of the horses without even seeing them; nor did he more than half hear Tag Klebold's sour comments.

A fiddlefoot has his pride, and it has to be a towering one because he possesses so little ammunition to back it up. Thus it was with this Bill Dawson, who held his freedom a fair exchange for the scorn which the settled and responsible men who hired his kind often showed him.

That, he could take; he had an unspoken scorn of his own for men of property, who would throw away the liberty of movement that was their common birthright in return for a few dollars in the bank. But against the humiliation of a horsewhipping such as the one he had just endured, pride had no defence. He knew he was either going to have to swallow that insult — or find some way to square it.

It was a sobering reflection for a peace-loving man. He had already got himself into enough trouble with Big S, not to need it made any worse by a private feud with Slater's range boss. In fact, if he knew where wisdom lay he would be pulling out of this thing right now.

He would tell Tag Klebold to stop this crazy rig long enough for him to get his saddle out of the back and his bay gelding untied from the tail gate. He would clear out of Renner Valley. Forget Slater, and Virg Noonan — and this rather unsavoury character on the seat beside him who was obviously as unscrupulous a crook, in his own small way, as the combined Trent and Big S outfits with which he claimed to be at war.

But then Bill Dawson touched again the rawness where Noonan's riding crop had broken the skin across his cheek. He felt again the falling of the blows, heard through the buzz of a punished eardrum the violent scorn of Noonan's words. And, remembering, he made no move but stayed the way he was, and let this wobbly freight rig creak on down the valley road with him, through the steaming sunlight of spring.

3

The cloud ceiling continued to break and lift. Once, over to westward, it split open for the dazzling white cap of Renner Peak to show as though floating, disembodied, above timbered lower hills; but presently the shift of the cloud mass hid the mountain's head again and one might forget that the big pile of rock and ice was there, somewhere behind that grey and shifting screen.

After a while the valley narrowed perceptibly, at a point where an intrusion of impervious granite had hampered the eroding action of the streams which formed it. The rock ribbed walls pinched close, and across the narrow waist thus formed stretched a four-strand fence of barbed wire, anchored at either end in crumbled talus boulders.

A wide double gate, hanging open, allowed the wagon road to pierce this barrier. And as they rolled through, Tag

Klebold shifted on the seat and drew himself erect, like a man who has just shed an invisible burden. 'That was the boundary,' he explained. 'Now we're in South Renner, and out of Steve Slater's territory — so long at least as the farmers can manage to hold him back to his side of the line!'

Bill Dawson frowned a little. 'I'm surprised they were even able to get a toehold. How did Slater happen to let them?'

'Well, I reckon he'd rather not have, if the truth was known. But there's limits to how far a man like him can dare to go — even with the local law safe in his pocket. When the farmers started leaking in, about a year ago, there was threats, and some fence-cutting and barn-burnings at night. But rumour has it the judge and the sheriff told Slater if he didn't go easy it could mean bad trouble for all of them; though they'd back him to the hilt, of course, if he could just whomp up some reasonable-sounding excuse for his dirty work.

'So it seems he's finally found it. Slater has always used this road for a drive-trail; now he says the farmers are violating their agreement to keep it open so his shipping herds can reach railhead. Also he claims they kill off his beef, trying to keep him north of the drift fence.'

Dawson said, 'None of it true, huh?'

'Those farmers ain't asking for suicide. Maybe one or two have butchered a Big S steer for meat, on occasion; but would they invite war by going back on their promised word, and ploughing up the drive trail?'

It certainly didn't seem reasonable, but Bill Dawson made no further comment; he wanted to see more of what was going on here before he formed an opinion . . .

A change was apparent as soon as they passed the wire barrier and moved southward of Big S graze. For suddenly they were in farming country, with land under the plough and fenced into fields and homesteads. The principal farms were strung along a clear-water stream that threaded the centre of the valley — new, neat-looking places, the buildings mostly temporary half-sod structures that would be replaced later. Dawson learned there were some score of families living here in the south valley, where they had followed their patriarchal leader, Tom McHail.

'This is McHail's,' the freighter said, as they pulled in sight of a place that looked better established than the rest, its buildings larger and substantially built of lumber freighted in from railhead. 'End of the road, for today; I contract with him to put me and my teams up overnight when I make this Renner trip. Not a bad arrangement, either. Miz' McHail, she sets a generous table,'

He turned his rig into a pasture beyond the farmhouse, and instructed his new man to water and then picket the horses out to graze while he himself walked over to the house. The job done, Bill Dawson sauntered in that direction, through the long golden light of sunset that slanted through the gaps of the tattered clouds.

They seemed to be not the only visitors here this evening, he noticed casually; a buggy and a number of saddle horses were tied to a hitchpost, and to spokes of the white-painted veranda railing. Bill spotted a pump by the back step and went around there to wash up. The cold water stung his sore cheek as he splashed it over face and neck.

An iron cup hung from a chain and he filled this, enjoying the clean, metallic tang of the water. He was trying to wipe his face upon his shirt sleeves when a voice said, pleasantly, 'Wouldn't you like a towel?'

He turned; he hadn't heard the opening of the back screen door, or her step as she came out upon the porch: a girl — a very pretty girl, dark and slender.

'Thanks,' said Bill Dawson, taking the towel. In doing so he saw the plain gold band on her finger. 'Very thoughtful of you, Mrs. McHail.'

He liked her quick smile, 'You must be thinking of my mother,' she said, 'I'm Jean Burke. We're already eating,' she added, holding open the door for him. 'Won't you step in?'

'I surely will.'

He gave her back the towel and moved inside. As with most farm homes, the big kitchen was the spiritual centre of this one and the roaring wood stove its blazing heart. A motherly-looking, grey haired woman turned from her work long enough to pile Bill Dawson's plate with food, and pour him a cup of coffee from the graniteware pot at the back of the stove. He thought the smile she gave him matched her daughter's.

Bill grinned his thanks and took the plate into a corner, where he set the steaming coffee cup upon a shelf and leaned his shoulders against the wall while he went to work on the food, standing. He had ridden grubline and sampled handouts across the face of a dozen states, and was a connoisseur of grub both good and bad. This ranked high.

Tag Klebold's bony frame was folded onto a high stool near the scrubbed-pine drainboard; he had already finished and was shoving shred tobacco into the bowl of a blackened corn cob. He made no offer to introduce the newcomer and Dawson had to fill in for himself, as best he could, the identification of the other people in the room.

Yonder stiff-shouldered, white-bearded man in overalls, seated at the end of the long trestle table that was covered with the litter of a meal's ending, was beyond question the leader of the farming group — Tom McHail himself. The others were men of the same work-hardened, sunbrowned stamp, whose names Bill Dawson heard now and then during the broken talk going on in the kitchen but without registering them.

Only one made a distinct impression on him — a dark haired, boyish chap with a clean and earnest look about him, whose name was Dave. The way the pretty girl liked to come now and again to stand behind him with her hand touching his shoulder, Bill guessed that he was young Burke, her husband — probably not long married either, and transparently in love. That, of course, would make him old McHail's son-in-law.

The visitors, Bill Dawson quickly surmised, were here at the McHail place for a reason. They had a serious matter on their minds and their meeting was very much in the nature of a council of war.

'I ain't surprised,' said Tag Klebold now, unhitching from his stool long enough to snag a stick match from a box of them atop the stove. 'I ain't for one minute.'

'I am,' declared Tom McHail, heavily. 'I would have said Jabez Trent was a strict business man, but a fair one. It's hard to believe he'd deliberately watch two dozen men ruined.'

Young Burke said, scowling, 'I'm afraid Tag's got it pegged. Trent is playing Steve Slater's game for him, to the hilt — and in this case he doesn't have to do anything but sit tight and keep the door of his warehouse locked. *He* won't lose anything.'

Jean Burke exclaimed unhappily,

'Surely there must be something — some way . . .'

'I dunno what it would be!' Tom McHail turned ponderously in his chair, put a sombre glance through the window that framed a tumult of cloud and sunset fire.

'My land is harrowed and ploughed,' he said, in dark musing. 'Just waitin' for the seed. It's the same with the rest of you — we've broken our backs, and our hearts, gettin' this valley ready for spring planting. And now, what are we supposed to do? See all that work go for nothing? Watch the plantin' time pass and our fields lie empty — while the seed we scrimped and saved for lies rotting in Jabez Trent's warehouse, and we know we'll never scrape together the money to buy another batch?'

He lifted a hard, work-calloused hand and let it fall, heavily, to the table top beside him. His bearded chin sank upon his chest, under the weight of black and discouraging thoughts. Nobody spoke; the silence was heavy except for the crackle of wood fire in the stove.

Bill Dawson speared the last morsel on his plate, scraped up the last drop of gravy. He said, in a voice that sounded startlingly loud as it broke the brooding silence, 'Real good grub, ma'am.'

A sharp glance or two, irritated by the irrelevance of this statement, lifted briefly as he moved across the scrubbed plank floor with spurs chiming and placed his piled dish and cup and silverware in the wreck pan in the sink. Then he turned to address the room, and this time his words were pointed to the subject that filled their minds.

'Don't aim to butt in,' he said, as he fumbled in a shirt pocket for tobacco sack and papers. 'But what you're saying kind of puzzles me. As I seem to gather, this freighter, Trent, has some bags of seed in his warehouse consigned to you folks, and he won't let you have them.'

Old McHail nodded shortly, not looking away from the window. 'That's it.'

'But how can he do that? Didn't you say it was already paid for?'

54

'That makes no difference.' McHail did turn towards him now, as though in exasperation at having to explain a situation that already had been thrashed over a dozen times and was painful to relate again. 'We're in debt to Trent, every man of us. Few of us have wagons of our own, and it takes a lot of loads to haul in the supplies you need to start farming, in this country. Besides which, Jabez Trent's rates ain't what you'd call low. Well, now he tells us we got to pay up or not another wheel rolls this way, short of a full cash settlement. And he's holding our goods that are in his warehouse, against that payment.'

'Still,' exclaimed Bill Dawson, incredulously, 'you would think a thing as perishable as seed — '

Young Burke cried, with a look of disgust: 'Why argue with *us* about it? If you feel like arguing, take it up with that pious old devil in Fair Play — and see how much good it does!' His fingers balled into a tight fist. 'Damn his soul, I'd like to — '

'Dave!' His wife put a hand upon his arm, and the corded muscles smoothed out, went lax. Hopelessness replaced the anger in Dave Burke's young, good-looking face.

'I was thinking of a court order,' said Bill, patiently. 'Certainly, any judge who understood the nature of the situation —'

A snort of disgust broke from one of the farmers. 'You're meanin' the judge in Renner City. Sure, Judge Hawkins understands the situation! He understands it just the way Steve Slater tells him to; and Slater's the power behind Jabez Trent.'

Bill Dawson made a small gesture of indifference. 'Well, all right,' he said. 'Don't mind me; I was just making talk. . . . Thanks, again, Mrs. McHail. It was right fine grub!'

He walked to the door, got his jacket and battered hat from the wall peg where he'd hung it on entering. But what he heard from Tag Klebold just then made him pause with one boot already shoving the screen open, ready to step outside.

'It ain't any of my business, either,' Klebold was saying. 'But if that seed belonged to me and I needed it bad, I think I'd find some way to take it — with a gun, if no other.'

'We'll not have that kind of talk,' responded old Tom McHail, promptly. But next moment Dave Burke was on his feet, facing the room in a blaze of angry defiance.

'And why not? I say it's time we did have it! We're men, ain't we? A man should fight . . . '

He stood like that, glaring about him as he reached up to sleeve an unruly lock of black hair from his eyes. Close beside him, his pretty wife had her fingers twisted together and she looked at him with face drained of colour. 'No Dave!' Her voice was little more than a whisper. 'You mustn't! You don't know what you're saying.'

Bill Dawson, in turn, looked over at the girl and he felt the stirring of an emotion that was strange to a tumbleweed rider like himself, unhampered by ties of responsibility or the solicitude of dependent love. His girls had been of the casual type to whom he was no lasting concern, whether he stayed or whether he drifted; and that had been all right with him. Now, however, he read the emotion in Jean Burke's face and in her voice, and he knew a strange and unwonted quirk of something very near to jealousy towards this lank, dark haired farmer lad — her husband.

Such a discovery in himself was a little disconcerting; but even more so was the impulse that made him withdraw his boot from the half-opened door . . . even as a silent, warning voice said, 'Watch it! You're not much good today at staying out of other people's troubles.'

Tag Klebold was talking again, gazing slit-eyed into a film of smoke from his corncob as though reading his thoughts there, aloud. 'It might not be too big a job if it was done at night. Trent's warehouse is in a deserted part of town, down by the tracks; with no guard but that one-armed scarecrow they keep for a night watchman. A quart of rye would put him out of the way.'

'Now, hold on!' Tom McHail scowled darkly as he looked from Klebold to young Burke. 'You're talking nonsense — both of you.'

His son-in-law turned on him. 'And why is it nonsense?'

'Why, there's at least three wagonloads of seed down there. You can't just walk in and carry that out under your coat.'

Klebold squinted into the bowl of his pipe, to see what was wrong with its draw. 'I got wagons,' he pointed out, absently.

'There you are! 'Dave Burke flung out an arm, triumphantly. 'Tag's willing to help us; aren't we going to do anything to help ourselves?'

Harris, one of the other men, seemed to catch fire with something of their own enthusiasm. 'The kid talks sense, Tom!' he declared, cutting off Jean Burke's quick protest. 'If Klebold will lend us the use of his teams, we can damn well do the loading.'

'Why, sure you can have the rigs,' said Klebold. He had decided his pipe was out of working order and he knocked the smoking dottle from it into his plate, stowed it away in a pocket. 'We can bring them up the alley behind the ware house, one at a time — shouldn't take more than a quarter of an hour to fill each wagon. Done quietly, there's small danger of anyone interfering.'

'But the wagons will be easy to trace,' McHail protested. 'You can't hide wheel tracks.'

Young Burke said, 'And what do we care? They're bound to know, anyway, who took the stuff. But it's ours! We paid cash, we have our receipted invoices. Trent has no legal right to do anything, should we change our minds and decide to haul from the railhead ourselves. Why, if there was decent law in this county we could walk, in openly and claim our property, despite any past due freight bills!'

'That's the truth, Tom!' Harris agreed. And another of the men nodded and said, 'I'm for trying it — when the only alternative is setting still and letting ourselves be ruined.'

Old McHail clawed at his white beard, in an anguish of indecision; and Bill Dawson could see him weaken beneath the arguments that were being hurled at him. The girl, obviously sensing that her frantic pleas were going to have no effect in changing Dave Burke's stubborn mind, had subsided now and haltingly backed away from him; and her mother slipped a comforting arm around her waist. At a moment like this, a woman learned she could hold little weight in the councils of her menfolk.

Then the old granger gave in, with a gesture of defeat.

'All right,' he groaned. 'If there was another way, you know I wouldn't stand for this. It's like you say, though: we haven't a choice.

'So make your plans, but make them good! If we're going to move, the earlier the better — tomorrow night. We haven't too much planting time left us.'

And this surrender on the part of Tom McHail apparently settled the issue . . .

In the big talk that followed, no one seemed interested in hearing any suggestions from Bill Dawson although he found himself tacitly included in their plans. He leaned against the edge of the door awhile, listening. Then, after a bit, he went outside and perched on the edge of the back stoop to build and smoke a quirly, while the voices poured through the door and the opened window above his head.

He eyed the coming of smoky darkness through young leaves in the head of a cottonwood tree beyond the barn, and he thought, 'I don't have to get into this. I owe these people nothing but a plate of grub!' There would be time later on, however, for declining a role in the enterprise; he didn't let himself worry about it, merely enjoying the smoke and the fine spring evening.

Afterwards, while enough light yet remained in the dusk to work by, he went out to the pasture for a final check on his gelding and the teams, to settle them on their pickets for the night. Cloud tatters were scurrying overhead, harried by a high wind that was scarcely felt, down here close to the earth. The night would be clear, he thought, and the morning also. Stars showed behind those ragged clouds, and yonder the big bulk of Renner Peak made a black and rugged outline.

The farmer's meeting had already broken up by the time Bill Dawson returned to the house, and the visitors were leaving. As he paused a moment under the cottonwoods to build another smoke, he saw a pair of figures emerge from the kitchen doorway and move slowly toward him through the darkness. It was young Burke and his wife. They halted, finally, only a few yards distant, and without wanting to he could hear their talk plainly.

'Oh, Dave! 'The girl's voice held a tightness she could not control. 'I'm frightened! Suppose something goes wrong! Suppose you're caught . . . '

'Now, honey,' the young man insisted, soothingly, 'nothing will go wrong. How can it? We've got this worked out, down to the last detail. We can count on Tag Klebold — you know that.'

'But to break the law!'

'It's only because we're forced to. Believe me, honey, if there was any other way — but you can see there isn't!'

Then the man in the shadow of the tree heard a sob and saw the dim figures merge together. Quickly he turned away, embarrassed, and put his back against the slim trunk of the cottonwood. He worked by feel to get his cigarette shaped, and when he had it finished he was relieved to see the two had moved on, without discovering him. Bill Dawson was frowning as he scraped a light against the tree bark and touched it to his quirly.

Klebold came out of the house, and Dawson walked over to join him. The freighter grunted, 'Oh, there you are. You better be seein' about the stock.'

'They're all put to bed,' Dawson

assured him. 'And I'm near ready to be, myself. It was a long day . . . '

Neither of them mentioned, just then, the plans for the following night.

Afterward, they sat for an hour talking with Tom McHail in the modest parlour of the farmhouse, with Mrs. McHail sewing silently under the lamp on the centre table. It was fine talk; the old farmer had lived a good many years, and he had lived them in earnest. Moreover, it appeared that in his younger days he had been something of a fiddle-foot himself. He recognized the signs in Bill Dawson, and he seemed interested in drawing him out concerning the country he had covered, the jobs he'd held. And, like most fiddle-foots, Bill Dawson loved to discuss such topics and did it fluently.

But fatigue caught up with him finally and left him yawning in the faces of his host and hostess, and quickly the McHails saw his trouble and brought the conversation to a close. There was an extra room, that had been their daughter

Jean's before she got married a few months previously. Stretched out on the old double bed beside the snoring Tag Klebold, Bill Dawson held sleep at arm's length while he had a clear-eyed view of the situation.

He liked these people . . . liked them a lot. But he still didn't think it was up to him to borrow any of their problems. He was probably in for enough merely by staying around and working for Klebold; especially, since he had promised himself a settlement with Virg Noonan for that quirting — at the very thought of which, even now, the welt that had been raised along the side of his neck seemed to swell and throb.

As for the planned raid on the Trent warehouse: he could see absolutely no reason to deal himself in on it — not even for the pretty face of Jean Burke. After all, Dawson reminded himself, she was another man's wife. Let Dave Burke worry about her.

Which was a comfortably cynical observation, making it possible to close his mind to any further stirrings of his conscience, and relax for now into welcome and greatly needed sleep . . .

4

Bill Dawson was already snapping the last team onto the chain before Klebold emerged from the kitchen next morning, all business and in a hurry to be off. 'We got to push 'em,' the freighter said brusquely. 'Want to reach Fair Play in plenty of time to arrange about tonight.'

Hurry or not, Dawson noticed he seemed to have a knack for being somewhere else whenever he might have been lending a hand with the bonerack teams.

'About tonight — ' Bill began after they were on the seat and the wagon was again heading down the trace. But Klebold was too full of his own talk to listen.

'This is a real chance,' he said, exultantly, 'to do ourselves a favour — as well as help those poor devils in the fight to hang on to their farms.'

Dawson looked at him. 'How do you figure? What do you get out of it?'

'Why, business, of course! Storage

fees, and all the freighting to and from this south half of the valley. Naturally, you can see they'll swing all their trade my way, after what I'm gonna do for them.'

The other said drily, 'I shouldn't think Jabez Trent would mind too much, losing a set of customers that can't keep their bills paid!'

'Oh, they'll pay, all right,' insisted Klebold. 'Once they're on their feet. Good lord, man! These people are only starting out. Just let them get in a cash crop or two . . . and how can they do that, without they got seed in the ground?'

'Sounds logical,' Bill Dawson admitted and quit arguing.

Towards afternoon the land grew rougher, as they got deep into the south end of the valley and the walls drew in. The road tilted up again, skirting the base of a granite cone that glittered with a million flakes of quartz. Then, climbing out of a tiny rock-floored cup, it went into a notch where a small wind moaned constantly, whipping the patched and

69

dirty canvas of the wagon cover. Here again the trail dipped sharply, and when they came out of the notch the basin lay behind and tumbled hills opened before them, to a flatland country beyond.

Through scrub timber the road shot downward, in a series of zigzagging, hair-raising switchbacks — curves so steeply graded that one almost could imagine that the very road might slide off the face of the perpendicular drop, taking the heavy wagon and teams with it.

And here Tag Klebold kicked on the brake and said, with a coarse grunt of amusement, 'Well, this is the Loops — the place where you have a chance to really show me what you can do with a freight team. So take her ahead, mister! She's all yours!'

The young man swallowed as he looked upon that dizzy stretch of up-and-down. He doffed his hat, ran a hand through coarse brown hair and dragged it on again, tugging the brim to settle it firmly.

'O.K.,' he muttered. 'I got nothing to risk but my neck, if you're blamed sure you want to take chances with your wagon. But just move over once, and let me at that brake! I promise nothin'.'

They made it without mishap, but Dawson's stomach still hadn't settled back into place entirely when they rolled into the town of Fair Play, along in the golden part of late afternoon.

This was a much larger aud prosperous town than Renner City, even if it wasn't the county seat. It had the railroad, for one thing; the twin lines of steel, under the late sun, were a bright streak that came in from the east and then curved southward, skirting the hills and Renner Peak. There were several blocks of business houses, with residences set behind them on gently rolling hill spurs. Beyond, lay rangeland.

Near the railroad tracks were the cattlepens, and onc large building that Tag Klebold pointed out: 'Trent's ware house.'

Dawson looked it over, deciding it was remote enough and that possibly the desperate plan of the Renner Valley farmers would really work if they got the breaks. But he still couldn't see why he should want any part of it, himself. There was no percentage in it.

They came into the town proper, past a large, fenced enclosure that held the high-bowed shapes of freight wagons, and a stock barn with the words, FAIR PLAY FREIGHT COMPANY, J. TRENT, PROP., painted in white letters across its red roof. As their own creaking rig heaved past the big gate, Tag Klebold leaned out and carefully deposited a gobbet of spittle in the wheel-marked dust.

Three blocks farther on, and down a side street, they reined in before a much smaller, very dilapidated building. There was a sagging barn at the rear, a weed-grown vacant lot beside it that boasted no fence at all. Another ancient wagon rested here, forlornly. KLEBOLD'S EXPRESS, announced crude lettering on a board nailed above the dark entrance.

The owner said, sourly, 'It don't look like so much — not yet. But I'm gonna grow, damn it! I'm gonna give them

72

high-and-mighty Trents a race like they never seen before. I reckon they'll stop laughin' at me, the day I close them out of business.'

He went on, in a completely altered tone: 'Well, take care of the outfit, and give the horses a good feed of grain, because they're going to work again tonight. I'll have my own hands full — got to locate another wagon, and a couple of extra drivers. Generally you can pick up a tramp at one of those track-side saloons who knows something about handling a team.'

'You better pick up three while you're at it,' said Bill Dawson.

Klebold gave him a hard look. 'You ain't backing out?'

'I never was in, that I knew of. I don't remember saying I'd have any part of it.'

'You draw my wages now.'

'Not for burglary, I don't.'

Klebold opened his mouth, then clamped it shut again, and the two men on the wagon seat exchanged a long and challenging glance. Something ugly in his voice, Tag Klebold said, 'You'd even like to tip the Trents off to what we're planning, maybe?' His bony hand began sliding back across the hard seat, towards the pocket of the mackinaw that lay behind him.

Idly, Bill watched him going after the gun. He said, with cold indifference, 'It's all right with me if you want to try for that iron. Mine's a whole lot handier. I don't even mind your insults, considering the source. You and your stinking little freight job don't mean that much to me, brother; and as far as I'm concerned, you can unhitch your own damn hayburners.'

With which he grabbed his jacket and turned to leap down from the wagon.

A quick word from Klebold stopped him. 'Hell, I'm sorry!' grunted the freighter, deciding to forget about the gun in his pocket. 'I reckon you wouldn't squeal on us. But this is a big job we're planning tonight and we counted on your help. You got a cool head. And even if I do manage to locate some teamsters to ride the wagon, chances are they won't be able to negotiate the Loops — not by night, certainly.

'If the job don't mean nothing to you, you might think for a minute about them Renner Valley farmers. We're their only chance, fellow. We can't disappoint them.'

'You're breaking my heart,' said Bill Dawson. And vaulting down to the dust he started to walk away.

He didn't get very far, however — not more than a couple of steps, before he slowed and then, with a grimace of self disgust, turned back. 'All right,' he grunted wearily. 'I probably won't be able to sleep tonight if I don't go through with it. Get down, and run along about your business. I'll see to the horses.'

Tag Klebold's bony face split in a grin of triumph. 'Get an carly supper,' he ordered, as he scrambled out of the wagon, 'and meet me here not later than seven o'clock. We'll start moving then.'

'Unless you can let me have a couple bucks advance,' Dawson reminded him,

'I'll have to eat oats with the teams. I'm broke.'

His boss sighed and dragged a slim wad of bills from his pants pocket, reluctantly peeled off a couple of them. But he was in a good mood as he went off down the street with a swinging stride of his gaunt legs; evidently he was highly excited over the prospects of that night's work. As for Bill Dawson, he was still wondering at his own easy gullibility, as he turned to his chore with the horses.

★   ★   ★

Now it was dark, with a sickle moon up the sky and the chill of early spring sharp in the night air. An occasional rattle of harness and stamp of hoof sounded in the darkness under a small stand of locust trees near the road from town, where Tag Klebold had gathered his battery of wagons and teams to await the nearing moment of action: three outfits, two his own and one other ancient ark of a vehicle that he had dug up from some-where.

Bill Dawson walked back and forth under the trees, swinging his arms. The chill of the night was in him, and the keener tooth of apprehension. Now that the thing loomed large ahead, the size and risk of the enterprise had him wondering again, peevishly, how he could ever have let himself be persuaded into it. It must have taken a soft heart — and a soft head.

Yonder by the wagons, whiskey gurgled in the neck of a bottle. The pair of derelicts Tag Klebold had roped in to drive the extra rigs were fortifying themselves against the chill. Bill dug his hands into the pockets of his leather jacket and swung about to stare at the town lights gleaming like scattered stars across the black and rolling land.

'Any time,' he thought, ill-temperedly. 'Any time at all.'

He judged it must be well towards nine o'clock. The delay was vastly irritating, stringing out nerves that were already taut enough from uneasiness.

But now, at last, the drum of a single horse came beating along the dark road, spurred at a fast gait. Quickly Dawson stepped forward, melting out of the trees. As the rider neared he knew pretty surely who it was, but he waited for Kiebold to rein in, calling hoarsely: 'Dawson?'

'Here.'

Tag Klebold came down from saddle. He was excited enough, and breathless as he made his announcement.

'We're started! The night watchman is out like a light; McHail's men have a guard stationed around the warehouse and Burke and two others are inside, waiting for you to bring up the first wagon.

'Roll into the alley behind the building and pull up by the double doors for them to load you. When you come past here on your way out, that'll be our signal to send in the next wagon. Wait for us at the Loops; if these bohunks I've hired can't maneuver them it'll be up to the two of us to get their rigs over the hump.

After that — clear sailing.' He slapped Dawson on the arm. 'Get going! You're holding up the show.'

'No sign of trouble, then? Everything's going smooth?'

'Smooth as silk. Now — roll!'

So Bill Dawson hurried to his wagon, climbed quickly to the driver's seat. Expertly, and with little waste motion, he yelled the horses into motion and got them straightened out and onto the road. Then, with a knot of tension balling tighter inside him, he was heading towards the town lights, appearing for all the world like a late-arriving freighter with business that was entirely legitimate.

He rattled across the loading switch and turned up the tracks towards the looming bulk of the dark warehouse. A figure moved in shadows at the corner of the building; a man's voice uttered sharp challenge. Dawson answered him and the Renner Valley man faded back, and a moment later his boot tromped the brake and the wagon halted in the black gut of the alley. The horses shifted, harness jingling faintly.

There was the sound of the double door sliding open on well-oiled runners. A bull's eye lantern shot its gleam out of the warehouse darkness, and showed him the vague figures of three men, hurrying forward. Even as Bill Dawson swung down the wheel he heard the thud of the first gunny sacks striking the floor of the wagon.

Everything had been well planned and the work went smoothly. Young Dave Burke was the man in charge, and under his prodding, the bags fairly flew into the wagon from where they had been dragged forward and piled just within the door. Dawson himself lent a hand, shouldering the heavy sacks and carrying them to dump into the rapidly filling box. Few words were wasted. There was little but the slither of hurrying feet, back and forth across the alley cinders; the grunt of panted breath as a man stooped and came up with a sack riding his shoulder. Once as Dawson and Burke passed each other in the beam of the lantern, the young farmer's sweaty face broke in a grin and he gave the bag he was carrying a proud slap. 'Russian wheat!' he grunted. 'The best there is. It cost plenty but it'll pay us back. Wait'll this stuff gets into that Renner Valley soil!'

He tossed it onto the load and stepped back, saying, 'Well, that's about a third of the pile — enough for this one. Pull out, fellow!'

The entire loading, with four men working on it, had taken a surprisingly short time. But the tension was still there in Dawson's belly and he was glad his part of the thing was nearly over. He would feel even better when he had this wagon out of town and on the road.

The farmers had extinguished their lantern and moved back into the darkness of the doorway, to wait for the second wagon. Bill climbed up to the seat, spoke to his teams. The wagon, weighted now, didn't rattle so badly as before when it rolled slowly forward, grinding the cinders of the black alleyway.

Then he had cleared the corner of the big warehouse — and heard the rush of running feet.

Dark figures came hurtling out of the shadows; a voice bawled loudly, 'Stop him! Grab those horses!' He came to his feet, fumbling for his gun and dragging it out. Up ahead the lead team reared in fright as hands grabbed at harness.

Bill Dawson, gun levelled, did not dare to fire into that dark confusion of men and animals. The wagon had stopped now, its front wheels cramping as the horses backed into it with frightened snortings. Cursing, he had turned to leap down when a sharp warning sounded:

'Don't move, you! I've got a rifle and you make a fine target up there on the wagon.'

The danger of it held him. And he was like that when the sound of guns and shouting began in earnest, in the alley behind the warehouse.

This didn't last long, really — a half dozen lashing shots, perhaps. But Bill Dawson, from his vantage point on the wagon seat, could look back and see the spears of gunflame, could trace the course of the running fight down the black alley, and to him it seemed as if the shooting would never end. Helpless to do anything about it, he could only watch and listen.

Presently, though, it was over, and through the fading echoes of the shooting a sudden drum of running horses began somewhere near at hand and quickly faded out.

Now men afoot came hurrying back through the alley; one called, 'They got away — three or four of them. I think we hit one, though.'

'Were any of you hurt?' anxiously demanded the person with the rifle.

'Naw, Miss Trent. We're all O.K . . . But what you got here?'

Now attention had shifted quite abruptly to the captured wagon, and to its driver. Someone said harshly, 'Yeah, we took one of the damn' looters — and a whole wagonload they nearly got away with. Get down, brother!' he added, to the man on the wagon. 'Throw down your gun and foller it.' Bill Dawson realized that he still held the Bisley; but there was certainly no chance to use it now. That chance was gone when he failed to answer the challenge of the rifle — a thing he might have done, except for his startled surprise at recognizing the challenger's voice as belonging to a woman. Now, at least a half dozen armed men had joined her there around the wagon and that settled any thought of resistance.

'Here,' he grunted. 'Somebody catch it.' With the gun disposed of, he came down to the ground himself, moving woodenly.

Immediately he was seized and held tightly — as though he would be foolish enough to try and break away from this superiority of numbers. Somebody said, 'Who is he?'

And a match was snapped to life against thumbnail, and shoved into his face. He blinked, jerking away from it.

'Nobody I ever saw before,' was the

verdict. 'Some tramp off the railroad.'

The match was shaken out; but by now somebody had produced a lantern and as it was set burning its yellow rays picked out the scene in eerie halftones.

Blinking against the after-image of the matchflame, Bill Dawson looked glumly around at the press of men who held him prisoner. The whole town, he thought, seemed to be coming alive to the shooting and excitement down here by the trackyard. Voices yelled across the night, and the mob around the wagon was beginning to swell with curious newcomers.

Then, Dawson saw the girl. She was a little thing, and young; her bright hair made a nimbus in the lanternlight and the ugly, shiny-barrelled rifle looked heavy and incongruous in the crook of her arm. But she was the boss apparently, of these tall men; and when she spoke they instantly fell silent, letting her have the floor.

'What have you got to say for yourself?' she demanded sternly.

Dawson shrugged. 'Don't look like there's much I can say. Except I hope your jail is comfortable.'

'What do you call yourself?'

'I hardly reckon that's important.'

She frowned, biting her lip; apparently she was both angry, and at a Joss what course to take with him.

Just then one of the men exclaimed, 'Hey! I know this wagon — it belongs to Tag Klebold. It's even got his name on it.'

'Klebold!' somebody echoed. 'What's the idea, mister? You swipe one man's outfit, to clean out another's warehouse?'

Somebody else had climbed up on the box for a look at its contents. 'Gunny sacks!' he announced, in a puzzled tone. 'That's all he took! Why, it looks like seed. Yeah — wheat! Bags and bags of wheat seed — '

'Well, what do you know?' grunted another. 'That's a damned funny thing to steal!'

Then the girl broke in, on a note of sudden decision.

'This is too big a crowd. Willie, go see if you can find the marshal. And, Chuck, you and O'Shay bring this man along into the warehouse where we can talk. The rest had better keep an eye on the wagon so nobody will be walking off with it before the marshal gets here.' She jerked her head at the prisoner. 'All right — you come along, mister!'

Bill Dawson went, having no choice. His guards shoved their way through the excited circle, each gripping an arm and one of them carrying the lantern that made grotesque, bobbing shadows in front of their moving legs. The girl with the rifle hurried ahead; by the time the men reached the warehouse entrance, she had found a lamp on a corner shelf and lighted it to show the neat interior of the big, barnlike structure, the boxes and crates stacked towards the shadowed ceiling.

'Close the door, Chuck,' said the girl.

Chuck blew out his lantern, hung it on a nail, and then rolled the door shut. After that the four of them faced one another in the big room, amid the litter of wheat sacks strewing the floor beside the entrance.

The redhead, O'Shay, suddenly exclaimed, 'Where's old Pete, anyhow? He ought to have been around. Hey! You don't suppose he's been — ?'

'Naw,' grunted the other man disgustedly, and pointed. 'Yonder he is — right over there on his bed. Stewed silly!'

Sure enough, on an iron cot against the far wall of the room, an old man lay sprawled amid rumpled bedding, asleep with toothless jaw dropped open. Beneath his one hand a whiskey bottle lay, partially emptied. O'Shay declared, 'I sure never thought he'd be one to go and get drunk on duty. Pete couldn't of done much to keep crooks out of the warehouse maybe, but he could at least have stayed sober.'

'I dunno about this.' Chuck walked over, shook the sleeping watchman, who gave loosely to it but made no sign of rousing. Taking the bottle from under the limp hand, Chuck pulled the cork, sniffed the contents. He shook his head.

'I dunno,' he repeated. 'Pete's got a capacity for rye. The amount of this he drunk shouldn't have knocked him out. There must have been something else in it.'

The girl made an exclamation, and it pulled Bill Dawson's eyes back to her. He saw now that she was indeed small, but that her body and her pretty face held strength. There was a firmness of will about her mouth and rounded chin. Probably this could melt to softness when she smiled, he thought; but she wasn't smiling now. Far from it.

'How utterly contemptible!' she cried, scathingly. 'To dope an old man's whiskey!'

There seemed nothing to say to that, especially as he agreed with her; and, of course, she wouldn't believe it if he tried to say he had not known anything about the knockout drops. So Bill kept his mouth shut, and merely looked at her, trying to meet the contemptuous stare of her unfriendly grey eyes.

'Yes, you certainly planned it well,' she continued in a biting tone. 'If a little boy hadn't noticed something wrong and run to warn the yard crew, you probably would have got away with this. But you're fairly caught, and if you're wise you'll answer my questions — preferably, before the marshal gets here.

'Who hired you to do this job?'

Bill Dawson grunted heavily, 'I dunno what you're talking about!'

'Aw, lemme paste him one, Lila,' growled O'Shay, doubling a massive fist. 'That ought to clear things up for him!'

'No, no!' She waved aside the suggestion, quickly. 'Mr. — whoever you are — why make things worse for yourself? Why try to cover up? Your friends ran off and left you to be captured; what do you owe them, now?'

Bill Dawson told her, 'I got nothin' to say.'

At that her manner altered again, became sharply angry. 'You may change your mind. Obviously, it was those shirt-tail farmers in Renner Valley who put you up to this. You surely don't think they'd turn a hand to save you?'

'Maybe Jabez ought to see the gent, Lila,' Chuck suggested darkly. 'He might know how to handle him.'

'No!' she retorted. 'Dad isn't to be bothered with this . . . '

The prisoner's head jerked a little. 'Not to be bothered, is he? Those ' shirt-tail' farmers aren't important enough, I suppose, for him to trouble himself about! That's very interesting!'

'You admit, then, they're the ones who hired you?' she lashed back, her face gone white with anger.

He caught himself. 'I admit nothing. But I've met those people, and I know what they're up against. I got an idea, too, what I think of any man who'd get another gent in a crack over his honest debts — and then deny him the one chance he has in the world of raising the money to settle them.

'How much good will it do Jabez Trent to let that wheat seed rot in his warehouse — when, in the ground, it would be the saving of a couple dozen families in Renner Valley?'

'All right!' growled O'Shay, darkly. 'You've talked enough.'

Still, the angry speech had hit home; Bill saw Lila Trent's reaction, saw her apparently trying for words to answer him and somehow unable to find them.

It was at this juncture that the big door rolled open again and two men entered-one of them a big-nosed, baldheaded man with a marshal's badge pinned to his coat, the other being the man called Willie who had been sent to fetch the officer. They had been running and were breathing hard.

The marshal took in the scene quickly, and turned on the prisoner. 'So this is the thief! A stranger, eh? What you been able to get out of him, Miss Trent?'

'Not — not very much,' she faltered.

'Oh, well; that's all right. We'll get plenty, before we're through with him — including all the names of his accomplices.'

A gun slid into his hand. 'I'm takin'

you to the city jail, buster. Give me trouble, and you might find a part of this gun-barrel gettin' bent across your skull.'

'Just a moment!' put in the girl, quickly. 'Please! We . . . I'll want to talk this over with my father. I'm not at all sure how far he'll want to carry it.'

'Sure, I understand. I'll just hold him overnight, and give you time to make your charges whenever you're ready. Tomorrow morning will be good enough.'

'Thank you.' She appeared troubled, Bill Dawson thought, as she turned to her men with hurried instructions. 'Have that wagon brought back here, to be unloaded for Klebold when he wants to come and get it. And someone had better stay the rest of the night while Pete sleeps it off.'

Chuck assured her,' Don't you worry! We'll take care of everything, Lila.' But it seemed to Bill Dawson that she hardly heard him — that her mind was filled with other things.

The marshal was prodding him, then. 'You can start walking! You're going to jail!'

'Maybe so,' retorted the prisoner, loudly, talking through him at the girl. 'But when you get me into a courtroom, just look out I don't do some sounding off that will really make a few ears burn. Yes, sir! That, I promise, I won't mind a bit!'

He heeled about, turning his back on the girl, and moved out ahead of the town officer.

5

Later, locked in one of the two small cells of the local calaboose, Bill Dawson toured the narrow cubicle and fumed with futile anger.

It was an all-embracing resentment that took within its compass every living being he had encountered during the length of this eventful and inauspicious day, and spared a generous share of disgust for his own stupidity. At each step of the way he had told himself, 'I'm not getting into this!' And here, certainly, he was in it — clear to his neck.

Hard to see what more could happen to him. Plainly, he was going to take the full rap for this business tonight. Tag Klebold was in the clear and could stay that way by dint of fast talking; and he surely needn't expect the Renner Valley farmers to do anything to help him. No, he was stuck — all by himself, and due for a charge of breaking-and-entering, plus anything else the Trents could make stick. They would probably throw him the works, in hopes of breaking him down and getting statements against the Renner Valley people.

His jaw set stubbornly, as he stood and glared at the dim square of barred window where a sickle moon hung low against western hills. So let them try it; they'd find out what kind of a war a fiddle-foot could put up — even though there was hardly much point in his protecting an indifferent bunch of strangers who had run and left him to his fate when their schemes went awry . . .

A strap-iron bed with an extremely thin mattress was chained to the cell wall beneath the window. Bill Dawson sat on this awhile, going over the mental treadmill and getting nowhere as he smoked down the last bit of tobacco he could shake out of his Bull Durham bag. Then, because there was nothing further to be done, he stretched out and made a half-hearted attempt at some sleep. It had been a long, tough day, and tomorrow certainly didn't promise any better.

He must have been more tired than he realized. Once relaxed, he slipped his hold on consciousness almost immediately.

The harsh voice of the bald-headed marshal, and the dazzle of a lantern shining in his face, was what brought him awake again. He sat up, blinking and groggy. It was still pitch dark; couldn't have been more than an hour or two later. His sleep-fogged senses clearing slowly, he registered what the officer was yelling at him:

'I said, hurry up! I ain't got all night to wait for you.' Bill Dawson stumbled to his feet, an arm lifted to ward off the punishing glare of the lantern directed into his eyes. 'What's up now?' he muttered, crossly. 'Going to take me out and hang me in secret? Can't wait till daylight?'

'I'm kickin' you out,' said the other, heavily. 'The Trents said let you go; so you sure as shootin' can't expect a free room on the city for the rest of the night . . . Start walking!'

'The Trents said *what*?'

'No charge!' the marshal explained impatiently. 'They got me out of bed to tell me the whole thing was a misunderstanding and I was to turn you loose — wouldn't even listen to argument.' He already had the door unlocked and he jerked it open. 'Make it snappy, will you? I'd admire to get back to sleep.'

Bill Dawson was thoroughly awake at last and the meaning of this turn of events had him sorely puzzled. Still, he would not waste time seizing the opportunity, once granted him; without further questions he moved out of the cell and into the tiny jail office, up front.

'Just a minute.' The marshal opened a built-in closet, took out the prisoner's jacket and hat and tossed them over. Bill caught them.

'There's still something,' said Dawson, 'I had a gun. Did somebody walk off with that, or do I get it back?'

The other gave him a sour look. 'I dunno why the hell you should!' he grumbled. But he went to a desk, pulled out a drawer and dumped the Bisley onto its scarred top.

'Just remember this!' he warned, as Dawson picked up the weapon and shoved it into holster. 'I'm gonna have a damn close eye on you, every minute you stay in this town. You've proved what you are, I reckon. The sooner you leave, the more I'm apt to like it.'

Bill Dawson gave him a long look, unperturbed. He said, coldly, 'Sure makes you grumpy, don't it — interrupting your sleep!' And with no other comment than that he turned and headed for the door, and the clean freshness of midnight dark.

Late as it was, he went first directly to the Fair Play Freight Line office, thinking that likely he would still find the Trents in session; but when he reached the big wagon yard and buildings of the company, he found them dark.

This disappointed him. He was in a bad mood and he loitered outside for some minutes while he worked to get his pent-up steam under control, being denied the release of venting it on Jabez Trent. At that hour of night he would probably have a hard time even finding anyone to tell him where the Trents lived. Well, there was tomorrow.

Meanwhile, the hour or so of sleep he'd had on that hard jail cot had only turned him groggy with tiredness; as the anger subsided and his head cleared he knew that the sensible thing to do was find a place to complete the rest that had been interrupted. And since he didn't have the price of a hotel room in his jeans, that left him one possibility — the hay-mow of Tag Klebold's stock barn. So he went there, through the sleeping town, bootheels striking echoes from plank sidewalks.

Klebold's fire-trap office was as dark as its neighbours; but when Bill Dawson crossed the empty lot next to it he saw with surprise that there was a light behind drawn shades at the rear of the building. He hauled up, eyeing the dimly etched windows. Then he walked over to the rear door and tried it, to find it locked.

As his hand fell upon the knob, a faint stirring within the room beyond fell quickly silent. He listened and, hearing no recurrence of the sound, tried the knob again. Then he laid his fist against the door, sharply.

'Who's there?' a voice demanded hoarsely.

'Dawson! Open up, Tag. I'm in no mood to be kept standing out here!'

'Who's with you?' Klebold demanded.

'There ain't anybody with me. Quit stalling and unlock this door.'

He heard the throaty gust of a released breath; then foot steps shuffled towards the door and the lock clicked. Dawson wrenched the knob, shoved the panel wide.

The office would be a dingy enough place, he supposed, by daylight — unswept, furnished with second-hand oddments, festooned with cobwebs in the dusty ceiling corners. Now, it was lighted by a lamp turned down so low that the starved flame laid a path of soot up one side of the glass chimney. Shadows danced weirdly in the gloom, and the air was bad due to the closeness of shade-drawn windows and the stink of smudging coal oil. Bill Dawson made a face. Shouldering in past the freight-line owner, he strode to the battered desk, thumbed the wick higher, and as the light strengthened looked about at the unseemly clutter.

The drawers of the desk stood open and overflowing with wildly scattered papers, some of which had spilled over to the floor and lay underfoot. Nearby, across a chair back, was a pair of saddlebags with the pouches open and hastily stuffed. A small box safe below the window had its door unlocked on messy contents.

Dawson looked at the freighter. 'Packing up in a hurry?' he commented drily.

Klebold had slammed the door and he stood with his bony shoulders against it, staring at his visitor. He looked in a bad way — his face slick with sweat, stringy hair plastered down upon his forehead. He wasn't able to form speech for a long moment, and then it was to croak, 'How did you break out?'

'Out of jail, you mean?' Bill's mouth quirked. 'So you knew they'd caught me — and you sneaked back to your hole, to try and grab up whatever you could and take with you before the law closed in. You must have been pretty sure I'd yell my head off!'

The man swallowed. 'I — that is, I — '

'Sure! Why shouldn't I talk? I get run into a thing that's none of my doing, and when trouble hits I'm the one that gets nailed while you and those farmers scatter like quail.' He shrugged. 'Well, you can unpack and come out of hiding. You're clear. So am I, for that matter. The Trents turned me loose.'

Tag Klebold couldn't seem to register this, immediately. Then he came forward and sagged onto the edge of the desk, his gaunt frame looking unstrung. 'I don't follow! Why would they do that?'

'Why, I've got a theory,' said Bill,

dumping the saddlebags off the chair and dropping into it himself. 'I think I scared them a little. I promised that girl a bad time if she got me into a courtroom on a breaking-and-entering charge. I said I'd give them a real earful — there's enough sense of decency left in this country that the Trents would show up pretty poor, once it was understood what they're doing to those Renner Valley farmers.

'Anyway, I figure she must have told Jabez what I threatened, and after that he couldn't hold still a minute until he'd routed the marshal out of bed and sent him over to turn me loose. Anyway, here I am. Got any smokin' tobacco?'

'A box of cigars there somewhere,' grunted Klebold. 'Have a drink, too, if you want.'

The other, already pawing through the clutter of the desk after cigars, paused to stab him with a sour look. 'No drink, thanks! Not if what old Pete got is any sample. I'll take mine straight — without knockout drops.'

His jibe was wasted, though, with no

apparent effect on Tag Klebold. With the sudden release of pressure from him Klebold had lost his queazy fright. He began touring the musty office, rubbing sweaty palms together as a new confidence began to build in him.

'This sort of changes the picture,' he exclaimed. 'I was expecting the law here any minute, hunting me — and wondering why they hadn't showed up already. Now, I understand!

'Well, and our plans tonight went to pieces on us; but there's no loss. Even the Renner Valley people aren't any worse off than they were.'

'One of them is,' Dawson corrected. 'One collected a bullet, or so I understand.'

'Yes, I guess that's right. Young Burke got it in the arm. He'll live, though.' Klebold didn't seem much concerned. 'Nothing for you to worry about.'

'I'm not worried.' For just an instant, the image of Dave Burke's pretty wife came to him, stricken with grief and anxiety for her husband; then he pushed it away. He added, gruffly, 'Apparently they weren't worried about what had happened to *me*!'

He stood up, taking the hat he had dropped on the floor beside his chair. 'So you can get to work and tidy things again. You're still in business.'

Klebold stopped sharp as a sudden recollection hit him and slapped cold water on his new-born exultation. 'My God! The wagon! They've got it, and they know it's mine.'

'So what? It don't prove anything against you. Tell 'em somebody hired the use of your outfit for the night. Or don't say anything at all — just go over to the Trents in the morning and claim it. If you want, I'll do it for you.'

'You?' Klebold looked up sharply. 'Hunh-uh. That's out. We've got to be careful that nobody connects us in a way. It's one thing for these farmers to steal their own property, and for you to help them. It's something entirely different for me — a business rival — to be mixed up in it.'

Dawson frowned. 'Still, if I'm gonna be working for you, it'll be hard to keep it a secret.'

'But you aren't working for me.' Tag Klebold dug out his roll of folding money, peeled off several bills and tossed them onto the desk. 'There — that pays you for your trouble, and a little extra. It'll be best all around if you were to fade out, right now; by morning, at the latest.'

'Oh!' Bill took the money, scowled at it, shoved it into a pocket. 'The sack, huh?' he grunted. 'Hell, I've sure had no luck since I hit this *range*!' He shrugged, and turned to the door. 'We'll see. Right now, I'm too far behind on my sleep to care much about morning. I thought I'd bed down in the stable, if you got no objections.'

'Of course not . . . go ahead.'

As Bill moved to the door, his ex-boss added, 'By the way, my bronc is still out there. Unsaddle him for me, will you?'

'O.K.'

In the barn, Bill Dawson found the spotted grey tied to a roof support, left there ready for a fast getaway as soon as Klebold had filled his saddlebags from the safe and desk in the office. Well, Klebold wouldn't be riding — not this night, anyway. Bill stripped leather and blanket off the animal and turned it out into the corral adjoining the sag-backed barn.

He thought glumly, at least he had some cash in his pocket — enough to see him on his way tomorrow to another range, another job of some kind. He'd watch his step, after this. He'd found now how a man could get involved, little by little, in the coils of a mixed-up business that was none of his doing. The coils had loosened, miraculously, and he was free. He'd take advantage of this, and clear out; he'd even forego settlement with big Virg Noonan for that quirting yesterday, in order to be sure that this mess didn't have a chance to tangle him up again.

Climbing into the mow of the barn, he found a warm bed in the hay and, with the decision made and settled, was quickly asleep.

★   ★   ★

Morning was clear and fair, with a pleasant breeze across the green land. A good day for riding, and the beckoning of new distances put its old excitement on Bill Dawson and had him eager to make trail. He came down from the mow, felt of the stubble on his jaw and decided to indulge in a town-shave for once, since he had the money in his pocket.

He gave his horse a feed of oats from the niggardly supp in Klebold's bin, as ammunition for the day's riding. Then he took a leisurely stroll over to Main Street, located a barber's shop by its striped pole and was soon stretched out under the sheet with the lather soaking into his beard.

Afterward, in the cleanest-looking of the town's three eat shacks, he ordered up a sizeable breakfast — cakes and black-strap, bacon and eggs and coffee. Eating slowly, he heard talk among the others lined along the counter stools about last night's excitement at the freight warehouse.

No one seemed to know very much for sure. Apparent the Trents had made no statement for publication, and the marshal — Ed Strawhorn — was also keeping a shut mouth about the whole affair. So it was mainly garbled, made-up stories that he heard, and he listened to them with a little of that smug superiority with which one overhears strangers indulging in guesswork about a matter of which one is acquainted with the details.

He finished his meal without haste, ready to ride as soon as he was done here. He was just sopping up the last of the egg and molasses with a chunk of bread when a finger punched his shoulder and, looking about, he saw the big-nosed town marshal standing behind him.

'As soon as you're through,' announced Strawhorn, with an officious scowl, 'I want to see you on your way out this town. You get me?'

Bill Dawson's jaw went tight, the cheek muscles bulging a little. The relaxed mood fled from him and his eyes, meeting those of the other man, turned cold and unyielding.

'Your wants,' he said, 'are the least of my worries!' And he turned back to the food.

Ed Strawhorn stayed where he was for a moment, his breath sour against Dawson's bent neck. He said nothing more, however, and after a bit he even moved away and strode out of the eat shack; but he halted out there, teetering on the edge of the plank walk, and it was obvious he was waiting for Dawson to emerge.

The taste of the food suddenly went bad in Bill's mouth. He dumped knife and fork into his plate and shoved it away, and leaned elbows on the counter while he considered. Damn it all! Now, why did that two-bit lawman have to go and shove his horn into this thing? Here he was, all ready and anxious to get his bronc from Klebold's stable and take the trail before morning got any older — and now Strawhorn had plainly made it impossible, unless he was to give this man the false satisfaction of having run him out.

So, impatience riding high in him, Bill Dawson stayed where he was and rolled an after-breakfast smoke with materials he'd bought from the tobacconist next door. Out of the tail of his eye he watched the plate glass and saw that Strawhorn was still waiting. It was obvious he had no intent of moving on, so with a grimace Dawson hitched off the stool and sauntered out to the street.

Strawhorn cocked a quick glance as he heard the screen door jangle. The marshal pulled out a big gold watch, snapped the case open. 'You got fifteen minutes,' he grunted heavily. 'Be out of town before that's up.'

'And supposing I'm not? What happens?'

'I don't think I'd wait around to find that out, if I were you.'

The watch case clicked. The timepiece disappeared into Strawhorn's pocket and without another look at Dawson the marshal walked away, across the rutted mud of the street. But once there he stopped and turned, to stand looking back. His whole manner said, 'You see, I'm not crowding you at all. I'm giving you plenty of room — that is, if you just follow orders.'

It was the wrong treatment for Bill Dawson, its effect exactly opposite to the one intended. Every bit of a high potential for stubbornness had risen to the top; he had been blocked now from his previous intention of doing the very thing Strawhorn wanted of him.

Fists clenched, he gritted out, 'All right! They want to push me, I'll push back!' And with sudden resolution heeled about and made directly for the one place which he had determined, after sober reflection, to leave strictly alone — the Fair Play Freight Line office.

He strode under the high gateway, crossed the yard and climbed two steps to the office doorway. This door stood open; he strode in and planted his fists on a railing and said loudly, 'I want to see Jabez Trent!'

The only person in the room — a

thin-faced clerk who wore a green eye-shade — blinked at him. 'I beg your pardon?'

'You heard me! I'm looking for the high mucky-muck that runs this outfit. I want him to call his pet lawdog off me or I'm apt to make some trouble.'

The man shook his head a little. 'You surely didn't expect to find Mr. Trent here?'

'Well . . . where, then?'

'Why, at his home. The big white place, two blocks north — with the locust tree in the front yard. You can't miss it.'

'Oh.' A little mollified, Dawson nodded shortly and walked out of the office and the freight yard, turning north.

As the clerk had said, it was easy to locate Trent's house — the largest in town, set attractively under a wooded slope at the very edge of Fair Play. Bill Dawson couldn't help contrasting it with the half-sod farm homes in Renner Valley, and the comparison caused his mouth to quirk with a species of anger.

He pushed open the gate, went up on

the porch and knocked — not gently. After a moment he knocked again, and then the door was opened by the same yellow-haired girl he had seen the night before.

Lila Trent didn't recognize him at first; when she did he read the surprise of it in her eyes. They were grey eyes, just off-blue — they would have to be so, to go with hair of that particular shade between honey and gold. She could do things with those eyes, probably, but they did nothing to Bill Dawson at that moment.

'What is it?' she demanded, on a caught breath. 'What do you want here?'

He repeated substantially what he had told the clerk. 'This pet marshal of yours,' he finished, 'this Strawhorn gent, said you had cleared me and had me kicked out of the jail. That's very damned generous of you, I'm sure. But I don't like being ordered out of a town, even when I've got no particular mind to stay. I came here to tell your father to call his dog off me or it's liable to get hurt.'

Her pretty face had got pinched and white with anger as he talked. 'Why, you — you're a boor!' she exclaimed, her tone a slap across the face.

'I imagine, by your standards, I would be. You probably figure I should thank you for being scared into turning me loose.'

'*Scared — ?*'

He shrugged. 'It's hard to believe Jabez Trent would do a thing like that out of the goodness of his heart — not from what I've heard about him, and the treatment he's given those Renner Valley people. It don't sound much to me as though he had a heart.'

She opened her mouth, shut it again. Then, resolutely, she shoved the door wider and said, in a tight voice: 'Come in here! I don't know why I should waste my time; but you make me so darn mad — '

Bill Dawson dragged off his hat as he moved past her into the bright, well-furnished living-room. 'You're actually gonna let me see this Jabez Trent?' he demanded, gruffly.

'Yes — the man with the horns, himself! Right through there, mister!'

Suddenly a little hesitant, Bill Dawson walked over to the white-painted door she indicated. It stood ajar; a faintly unpleasant odour tingled his nostrils as he approached. Then, beyond, an uncertain voice quavered: 'Lila? What's wrong now, girl?'

'Company, Dad!' She reached past Dawson, gave the door a little shove so that it swung wide and offered him a view of the wasted, white-haired figure propped against pillows in the big bed, arthritic hands knotted before him on the covers, a seamed and hollow-cheeked face turned anxiously towards the door.

Lila Trent announced coldly, 'This is my father . . .'

6

For a moment, staring at the invalid, Bill Dawson could not find his tongue. Here, he noticed, the smell of strong medicine and of illness was overpowering . . . the window closed, the shade drawn to lay a half darkness over it. This must have been the library before being converted into a sick room. The shelves rose to the ceiling, book-lined. There were books on the bedside table, and one lay open across the wasted limbs of the man in bed. He must be considerable of a reader.

Now he peered at Dawson from deep-set eyes. 'You wanted to see me, young man?'

The visitor swallowed. Lila Trent spoke ahead of him. 'This is the one, Dad — the man at the warehouse last night. He says he's here to make a row.'

'I see . . . Step in, won't you, sir? Have a chair. Sorry I got to receive you like this, but — ' The old fellow tapped a bony finger against his chest. 'Took pneumonia, a year ago — just a touch. Shouldn't have amounted to anything, but I'm ashamed to say it came near to knocking me out.'

'Ashamed!' cried his daughter, indignantly. 'You know what the doctor says. You've given your life to building a freighting business . . . doing the part of a hundred men in opening up this country. All the years of exposure, without thinking of your body . . . it's no wonder, when trouble came, you went under with it. The only wonder is that you haven't died!'

The invalid stopped her with a tired smile and a lifted hand. 'She's my trumpeter,' he told the visitor. 'You'll just have to excuse her, Mr. — ?'

'Dawson . . . Bill Dawson.' He blurted the name almost without realizing. So far, this interview was going completely otherwise than he had planned it. He found words hard to come by; this kindly, educated man was so far different from the hardhanded freight-line boss he had

119

expected to see.

Trent prodded him, gently. 'You have something on your mind? Something, I suppose, to do with last night?'

'That's right — about last night.' Bill plunged ahead with it. 'About those Renner Valley people, too, while we're at it. You're not what I pictured; you don't seem like the kind who would — would — '

'Persecute them for their debts?' Jabez Trent finished for him, quietly. A sombre cast came over his pallid features and he lowered his eyes to the twisted hands in his lap. No one spoke for a moment, in the oppressive silence of the sick room.

'It's a terrible thing — to be in debt,' the old man said then. 'It can warp all a man's ideas. I suppose it's got those farmers in Renner Valley picturing me as a sort of fiend — like a spider, sitting here in my web — ' He indicated the book-walled, musty room, and the big iron bedstead ' — and sucking the life out of them. But it can do even worse things than that. It can make a man close his eyes to the needs and rights of other

120

people. I guess that's what it's done to me.'

'You?' exclaimed Bill Dawson, a little incredulously. 'In debt?'

'A year of sickness is a pretty expensive indulgence young man.' The other's smile was filled with bleak sadness. 'Frankly, it was one I couldn't afford. The cost of doctors and medicines, and the wasted time, drained all my cash reserves. Meanwhile the business has to go on . . . rolling stock and teams have to be replaced, and — the details don't matter.' He waved them aside, as though the burden of those dreadful months was a thing not worth discussing.

'The point is, I had to borrow — and in this country, that meant borrowing from Steve Slater of Big S. No bank would touch me, because they were sure I would die in a few months. Well — I haven't.' His mouth quirked in a humourless smile. 'I've hung on, no good to myself or anybody else. Lila, here, runs things almost singlehanded, except for what little help and advice I can give her — '

The girl broke in: 'You mustn't say that, Dad! All I've done has been to take over some of the bookwork.'

'Call it so, if you want,' he told her briefly, and turned again to Dawson. 'Anyway, there's the situation. And when you owe money to Steve Slater, he keeps track of it . . . The first of his notes falls due next month. I've been hoping for an extension; but he doesn't much like the shape of the business, I'm afraid, or the books. We're carrying too much credit, he says.'

Dawson finished for him, drily, 'So friend Slater breathing down your neck is your excuse for squeezing out the Renner Valley farmers? That's the picture you're giving me?'

'I'm afraid so. I've told you I'd been blind; but last night — and what Lila passed on to me of the things you said — finally opened my eyes. I'm very glad you came here today, young man; because I feel I ought to thank you. And the Renner Valley people . . .' He glanced at his daughter. 'I'll let you tell him.'

'The wheat is being loaded, now,' she said, her voice without warmth, her grey eyes cold as she looked levelly at Dawson. 'It goes up to them as soon as we can deliver it. Now — are you satisfied?'

Bill stared a moment; then came lumbering to his feet, abashed. 'If this is true, I — I guess I owe a few apologies!'

'Don't!' Jabez Trent stopped him, quickly. 'You made plain talk — and it took that to make us realize how we'd sold out to Steve Slater, and how much wrong we'd done. Our names are pretty much linked with Slater's nowadays, I'm afraid. We don't want to let that continue.'

'Still, to cross him like this — '

Jabez Trent let his stooped shoulders lift, and then fall, tiredly. 'We'll make out. I don't know how, but we'll meet his notes someway. It will mean retrenching — cutting back almost to the place I was twenty years ago — starting practically all over again. But, at least our hands will be clean. For myself, I don't care. I did hope, though, to leave better than this to my girl.'

She crossed to the bed, quickly, and took his head against her breast. 'Oh, no, Dad! 'Her voice had the catch of a sob in it. 'I've told you, it doesn't matter. Please don't ever say that again.'

In acute embarrassment, Bill Dawson was stumbling backward towards the door and only wished he could get away from there without being noticed again. The girl's eyes, bright with tears, turned to him above her father's white head as he mumbled, 'Well, I guess I've been answered. I promise I won't bother you folks any more.'

Lila Trent said, 'About Marshal Strawhorn — '

'Forget him! He sort of got my goat, but it wasn't worth making a fuss over.' He added, 'As far as Tom McHail and the farmers are concerned, I don't think you'll regret playing fair with them. They'll pay their bills — to the dime. All they need is a chance.'

'I know . . . I know that.' The sick man nodded. 'I've never really been afraid they wouldn't.'

'Unless, of course,' Dawson finished, 'Steve Slater starts a war and wipes them out. Well, good day, folks. I guess I can find the front door by myself.'

He got away, then, dragging on his shapeless Stetson as he left the Trent place with that strange interview swirling in his mind, and his judgments on a good many things falling into a totally new perspective.

Somehow, he was unable to doubt the sincerity of old Jabez Trent; and the girl possessed a certain native honesty to which even his anger of the night before hadn't entirely blinded him. He had to believe, now, that the truth of this whole mixed-up business was as they had told it to him, and that Jabez Trent's enemies were wrong in classing him in the same category with Steve Slater.

After all, McHail and the other Renner Valley people hadn't known Trent as he was before the pressure of illness and debt came upon him. Bill Dawson could guess they would be due for a real surprise, shortly, when they heard news of the old man's decision . . .

Meanwhile, the important thing was that he still lacked a job, with a good many miles to cover between here and another place where he might find one. He'd have been tempted to ask the Trents except that they were cutting their crew, not hiring. So he went through the town straight towards Klebold's to get his horse and take the trail that he should have been riding an hour ago.

Somehow, after that conversation, his annoyance with Ed Strawhorn seemed a petty matter and it no longer concerned him, now, whether the marshal thought he had chased him out of town or not. Strawhorn was, in fact, just about the farthest thing from his mind.

A man in overalls and heavy farmer's shoes was riding away from Klebold's. He called Dawson's name and reined over quickly, and Bill saw that it was Frank Harris — one of the farmers who had been involved in the fiasco at the warehouse the night before. A yellow-haired man with face burned the colour of brick by sun and wind, he leaned from his patched saddle to exclaim:

'I'm right glad to see you! I was just talking to Tag and he said you'd left town. Us folks was worried about you, knowing you'd got in trouble with the law and on our account; they sent me back to find out if there wasn't something we could do. It's a real relief, findin' you free.'

A measure of astonishment filled Dawson, hearing this — and a kind of shame. He'd thought these Renner Valley people had left him to his fate, their own skins being saved. Thus refuted, he hardly knew what answer to make.

He blurted, 'I understand young Burke got it in the arm. Anything bad?'

'Oh, no. He lost some blood, but it was a clean hole and we got it patched good enough . . . Anyway, I want to say, 'Thanks', for your help last night; and if we weren't as short of cash as we are we'd like to repay you.' He reached towards a hip pocket of his overalls. 'We did take up a little purse, thinking it would help hire a lawyer. It ain't much, but still we'd like you to have this . . . '

'Forget it! Use the money to pay the Trents something on account — with my compliments.' He added, 'I just learned that they've decided to let you have your wheat.'

Harris nodded. 'I know. I also know whose talking it was convinced them. That's more thanks we owe you.'

He held out a calloused hand, and Bill Dawson shook with him. Afterwards, the Renner Valley man rode on, at a slow lope. Bill watched him go, and then went around to the stable at the rear of Klebold's place and set to work throwing gear onto his bronc.

The best part of the morning had already been used up, at one thing or another, and it was not far from ten o'clock.

But he didn't regret the lost hours; his talks with Harris and the Trents had been worth the time they took.

He put the bridle on and then led the bay outside, to where the saddle blanket had dried overnight across the top pole of the feed corral, with his battered tree racked beside it. Dawson spread the blanket in place, was smoothing out the wrinkles when over at the office a swollen window opened with a squeal and Tag Klebold yelled at him.

'Now what?' Bill Dawson grunted, and left his horse and walked over there.

Klebold looked excited. 'A good thing I caught you! There's a chore I won't have time to handle.' He flourished a yellow telegraph form. 'A shipment of mining equipment, due on the ten-thirty-three — and the manager of the Silver Queen is in a rush to get it. I want you to meet the train, load that shipment and get it on the road to Renner City — pronto!'

The other scowled. 'Now, wait a minute! I wasn't workin' for you any more. Remember?'

'Yes, yes — I know.' Klebold brushed aside the objection. 'This is an emergency — I got other business that needs tending. I'll give you the invoices and the rest of the papers; you have a wagon and team ready when the train rolls in — pick up some of those station loafers to help load you. Operations at the mine are being held up until the machinery gets there.'

'I thought you didn't want to be identified with me? 'Dawson objected. 'I thought it could get you into trouble.'

'That's a chance I'll just have to take. From what Frank Harris tells me, there won't be any trouble with the Trents over last night. I figure I can write that off the books.'

Dawson said, 'I suppose you heard, then, about them letting the farmers have their seed? At least we got what we aimed for.'

The other made a sour face. 'Who says we did? There's not a chance, now, of those farmers switching their business over to me. They'll be tied to the Trents harder than ever — which sure as hell ain't what I was aiming at . . . Well, forget it. You'll take care of that shipment?'

'Why, I just don't know. This here is the damnedest country for a gent to keep straight whether he's got a job or not. If I'm hired, then O.K. — but for Pete's sake, make your mind!'

'You're hired,' Klebold assured him, briskly. 'Come on in and I'll fix you up with those papers.'

'I'll have to strip my bronc first.'

'Make it snappy, then. I'm in a hurry.'

Bill Dawson was sure the bay gave him a look of bewilderment as he went back to it and began pulling off the gear. He said, with friendly slap on the sleek neck, 'You and me both, pony! Our employment status changes by the hour. Me, I never did care much where I worked or who I work for — but the uncertainty of this job is beginning to get my goat.'

Still, it was a job, and as good as any. So he hung up bridle and blanket again, put his gelding into the pen, and rolled a smoke as he legged it towards the office to resume once more his interrupted duties as teamster for Klebold's Freight.

★   ★   ★

At ten twenty-five, Bill Dawson brought a wagon and team around to the rear of the yellow-painted railroad station, only to learn that the freight would be ten minutes late in arriving. So he walked back and forth along the wooden platform, looking at the blue sky with its dotting of small clouds and waiting for the first long moan of the whistle to come sounding across the hills.

Before the big engine came in, panting its breath of hot metal and steam and making the ground tremble to the drive of its powerwheels, he had a crew of platform loafers organized and ready to fall to work the instant the freight car could be unsealed and cleared for emptying.

In good time the job was done, and his helpers paid off. He was just about to climb to the wagon seat when he saw Marshal Strawhorn hurrying towards him across the cinders.

Dawson made a face. 'I plumb forgot about *you*! 'he grunted, and leaning an elbow against a spoke of the big front wheel waited impatiently for the marshal to come up.

Strawhorn came, yelling and furious. 'I told you what would happen if you didn't leave this town!'

'You did not!' Dawson retorted. 'You made some dark hints, but you never come right out and said. So curiosity got the better of me, and 1 just stayed around to see.' He straightened, letting his voice harden. 'All right, tin star put up or shut up! I'm calling your bluff. Do what you've a mind to, but do it quick; because I got to get this outfit on the road!'

The marshal turned red, but he didn't blow up. Some thing else had caught his interest. His glance ran sharply over the wagon and team, and the name of Tag Klebold stencilled on the box. His eyes narrowed. 'What's going on? Stealing some more freight, maybe?'

A small crowd had collected. The station master, an old man with black sleeve protectors on his arms, answered. 'He's working for Klebold, Ed. He had papers and the authority to pick up this load and run it to the Silver Queen.'

'And they're in a hurry,' Dawson added. 'So if you'll just stand to one side, I'll be on my way. What the hell have you got to beef about, anyhow? I'm leaving town, ain't I?' He added, 'Of course, I'll be coming back, too.'

Saying which, he turned, deliberately, and climbed to the seat without Strawhorn offering interference. He uncoiled the long whip, kicked off the brake.

'Hey! Wait a minute!' yelled Strawhorn, as the thought struck him. 'If you work for Klebold, what does *he* know about that business last night?'

'Why don't you ask him?' Dawson called back; and then with a shout and a flashing of the long whip across the backs of his horses, he set the big wagon into motion.

Strawhorn started running, but it was too late. The wagon had picked up speed already and it rolled right away from him, rattling ponderously across the tracks as it headed for the road to Renner Valley.

Looking back, Bill saw the marshal come to a halt and stand, baffled and helpless, in the settling dust of the broad wheels. It made him chuckle a little. He figured this evened the score a little, between him and that loud-mouth, Ed Strawhorn.

7

For all the poor quality of this team and wagon, Bill Dawson managed to keep up a good pace. He had to; he was getting to a late start, if he was hoping to make the Loops before nightfall.

Plain in the dust of the road cutting ahead of him towards the hills, he could see tyre-marks of another freight rig. A Trent outfit, he remembered, had passed the station while he was busy loading, and it would be only a half hour ahead of him; he thought he might even be gaining on it some. He flexed the long bullhide whip, wondering if he had a chance of passing.

That would be something to talk about — overtaking one of the Trents' handsome wagons with this crowbait outfit. But then he decided it was out of the question. Most likely he'd only get close enough behind the other teamster to eat his dust all the way into Renner

Valley — and there'd be no pleasure in that.

So he dismissed the idea and settled back, letting the teams take their own speed; no use to burn them up in a futile wagon race, when they ought to be saving something for the tough ascent of the Loops switchbacks.

The foothills began to lift towards the timbered wall beyond which lay Renner Valley. The sun was warm overhead, the cloudflecked sky deep blue beyond the shifting pattern of green-gold treeheads. Time ran along. In mid afternoon, the steepness of the terrain began to increase sharply, and then timber fell away and directly ahead was the hairpin twisting of the Loops, up the face of what seemed almost a strictly perpendicular barrier.

If anything it looked worse, down there, than it had yesterday from above.

Sizing it up, Bill Dawson vented a low whistle, and pulled his outfit to a halt so as to give the horses a rest. One boot on the brake, he dragged off his battered Stetson, ran a bandanna around the sweatband as he squinted at the face of the steep slope.

Far up there, a yellow smear of dust was crawling slowly along one of the higher levels of the switchbacks. He knew that would be the Trent wagon, though he couldn't see the rig itself because of the dotting of stunted juniper that screened the cliffside.

Dawson watched the slow progress of that feather of dust, figuring he would just as soon not tackle such a climb with another outfit ahead of him. Any small mishap, and a team and wagon could lose the trail entirely — with nothing between them and the bottom to stop them, except for the scraggly scatter-ation of growth. And someone else, below, could be swept along with it to his doom . . .

The crack of a six-gun sounded, flat and far away.

Bill Dawson jerked up on the seat, jarred by the sound that had come and gone so quickly, without warning and without echo. He noticed all at once that the moving feather of dust had settled; the wagon and team causing it had come to a halt. And while he considered, frowning darkly, he heard a second shot — this time, the distinctive and unmistakable voice of a rifle.

He waited no longer. Hardly thinking, he had vaulted down from the wagon-seat and was running forward to the near leader, which was the likeliest of the six-team hitch. Hurriedly he ripped the harness from it and, without a saddle and only the headstall to guide it by, vaulted onto its back and kicked it into a run.

More gunfire came down to him from the stalled freight rig above; Dawson shipped his own Fisley, gripped it as the scrawny nag between his knees started at a labouring run up the looping switchbacks.

The Trent driver was in trouble up there, obviously; and though Bill Dawson was no hero he did not stop now to weigh considerations of personal danger, or personal concern. The tawny road flashed beneath him as he climbed, the bronc's shod hoofs spurting dust. One by one the sharp curves dropped below.

This horse had no bottom at all and was already faltering, its strength quickly draining; foam dripped from its muzzle and it had to dig in to make the heavy going at the steep turns. Yet Dawson punished it forward, relentlessly, making the animal pour out its last reserve; for he knew he was needed up there — needed desperately.

Still, the labouring nag could not make the last steep turn. It stumbled and went down, heavily, its rider barely managing to leap clear and avoid being pinned. One look at the exhausted horse and he knew there was no thought of getting it back upon its legs; he didn't waste time trying. He turned away instead and started off on foot, cutting directly across the neck of juniper-covered slope and making for the stalled wagon, whose top he could see just yonder above the stunted, twisted trees.

Gunfire was steady up there; he judged

there were close to a half dozen weapons working, including the rifle. Now as he made the tough climb through loose soil and scrubby timber, Bill Dawson saw the situation.

It was a Trent wagon, all right — the off wheeler down and thrashing in harness, a leg bullet-smashed, and its team-mates tangling and rearing with terror. The driver had the rifle; he was inside the wagon, keeping low within its protection and firing through the forward bow. His enemies appeared to be ensconced in the rocks and scrub growth above the road, opposite from where Dawson had held up for his quick surveyal.

The attackers were keeping to cover, respectful of that hidden rifle. There was only a dark glimpse of movement now and then against the grey trunks and olive-green foliage of the stubby trees, and the occasional flash of a gun or lift of black powder smoke to indicate where they were hugging shelter. Bill Dawson counted three. He wondered at their strategy; the canvas showed the tearing of the bullets, but the box walls seemed to be holding against the lead. He couldn't see what the trio thought they were accomplishing — until suddenly the shape of it became clear.

Yonder he had glimpsed a fourth gunman circling cautiously — moving through the growth to come in on the blind rear end of the wagon. His three companions, Bill saw now, were giving him cover with their steady fire. He was out of concealment into the road, darting forward at a crouch. The canvas cover would prevent whoever was inside from knowing of this danger.

Bill Dawson, boots braced in the loose soil, lifted his gun. 'You!' he shouted.

His challenge carried the ten yards and the figure made a startled whirl, seeking for him. Dawson saw that the man's face was covered by a dark neck cloth; then he fired.

His shot missed. The masked man answered it, and Bill felt the tug of the bullet as it sliced through the material of his jacket sleeve. He worked the trigger a second time, and his opponent went backward, hard, against the tailgate of the wagon. Dawson started towards him at a run.

The man had dropped his weapon; for a moment he sagged against the wagonbox, but then he gathered his bullet-shocked strength and pushed away from it, staggering. Dawson yelled at him to stop, but the man kept going, falling down once, only to get his legs under him again somehow and go lurching off across the roadway, dripping blood into the dust, reminding Bill of a stepped-on spider's frantic effort to escape.

Dawson could have tallied him with another bullet but he held back, repugnant to shoot a wounded man who was running away. And now the men in the trees yonder realized that he was in the fight and one of them threw an angry bullet at him, that slapped into the wagon timbers as Bill Dawson dived into its shelter.

He scooped up the gun dropped by the man he had plugged and, pressed flat against the tailgate, flung his shots two handed, trying to target the powder smoke that blossomed in shadows under the dwarf junipers.

Once he saw a hat go spinning, heard the squawk that broke from its wearer. Up in the wagon, it seemed to him the rifleman was working harder, no doubt encouraged by this arrival of unexpected aid. Suddenly the attackers must have reached the conclusion that they had drawn a blank here; all at once they had ceased fire and were starting to withdraw.

Bill Dawson was not foolish enough to go after them, and they kept too well to cover for him to find a target. He stayed where he was, therefore, guns ready; and presently hoofbeats started and the four riders flashed into sight, briefly, on mounts that had been concealed beyond the junipers.

They sped away up the curve of the switchback trail, one riding close to the stirrup of the wounded man so as to keep him, sagging and swaying, in the saddle.

Bill Dawson loosed a couple more bullets but could not tally; and then they were gone. He thought it unlikely that they would be back.

'All right,' he called into the wagon. 'That's it, I reckon.' And he was walking around to the front of the box when Lila Trent came swinging down the big wheel, clutching her smoking rifle, her pretty face pale and wild with the horror of what she had been through.

He hauled up, staring. 'You?' he cried, hoarsely. 'I never dreamed — but, of course, that rifle — '

And then he was hurrying forward to catch her — clumsily with a gun still in each hand; for he thought she looked on the verge of collapsing.

'It — it isn't anything,' she murmured faintly. ' I'll be all right. Only — ' The long gun drooped from her hand. Bill tossed his own weapons into the dust and his arms tightened around her, drawing her against him. She didn't resist. She was tired — tired through, and strung out by fright and the relief of her terror's ending. She placed her head against his shoulder and went limp within the protection of his arms.

'They were going to kill me!' Her voice was muffled by sobs, and by his jacket as she buried her face against him 'They talked about it — they meant to drive the wagon off at the turn and let it smash up as though it had been a accident — '

'But you spoiled that for them!' he exclaimed, proud of her courage and presence of mind. 'With your rifle, you sent them hunting cover like rabbits.'

She shuddered, in his arms. 'That's when they started shooting. I — I couldn't have held out very long. If you hadn't come when you did . . . '

Bill Dawson remembered the one who had crept to the rear of the wagon without her noticing, outflanking her, and he had to agree. It had been close, all around. A few minutes' delay on his part, and the story could have had a different ending.

But now Lila Trent had recovered from momentary unsteadiness. As he released her she moved quickly out of his arms, plainly flustered, and he said to cover a moment of embarrassment, 'Did you recognize any of them?'

'No. There were four — all masked. The leader was big, but that was all I could tell.'

'Brands on their horses?'

'I — didn't notice.'

He leaned then to get her rifle and hand it to her, and to pick up the two weapons he himself had thrown into the dirt. The captured six-gun he shoved into his waistband and afterwards, blowing the dirt out of his own Bisley, walked forward to see about the teams.

They were badly tangled in their harness, though subsiding now from the terror of the gunfire. Bill spoke to them, slapped a dusty flank or two, and bent to consider the hurt wheeler. The horse rolled pain-filled eyes. What was perhaps an accidental shot had smashed a foreleg and there was nothing to be done for it. Bill spoke soothingly to the suffering animal, and then, grim-faced, did the finishing job with a bullet from his gun.

He went back to where the girl waited, leaning against the wagon's big front wheel and still pale with shock. 'You'll be shy a horse, now,' he told her. 'I may be, myself, if I've killed the bronc I rode into the ground trying to get up here in time to help. But once across the Loops, the worst is over; and if we have to we can hitch our wagons tandem and throw what's left of our teams together.'

She was looking at him, in plain incomprehension. 'Your team — and wagon?'

'It happens that we're in the same business, Miss Trent. I'm working for Tag Klebold . . . signed on this morning, after talking to you and your father. Taking a load of mining machinery up to Renner City for him.'

'Mining machinery! That couldn't be the Silver Queen consignment, surely?' And at his nod her face darkened with anger; this must be her first word of Klebold's stealing the account.

Bill Dawson wanted to change the subject. Pretending not to have noticed anything in her manner, he said, 'I thought you only did the book work for your company. Where did you learn to handle a team and rig?'

She shrugged. 'Dad taught me — years ago.' She was distant, a little hostile towards him now. 'As we told you this morning, we're going to have to cut back our crews if Steve Slater demands payment on the notes he holds against us. And also,' she added, bitterly, 'if Tag Klebold manages to go on taking our best accounts out from under our noses. So I'm bringing the first load of seed up to the Renner Valley farmers, myself.'

'There's seed, in this wagon?' Bill Dawson studied the canvas-topped rig with narrowed, thoughtful eyes. He had already suspected as much, and it tied in with another theory of his own. 'The big man,' he prompted, suddenly. 'The leader of them that stopped you — would you say he was big like Steve Slater? Or more on the order of Virg Noonan?'

The girl had started to turn away; she came around again, staring at him hard.

149

'Do you realize what you're suggesting?'

'Why, I hardly reckon Big S would stop at anything, to prevent delivery of this seed. Without it, the farmers are ruined — licked.'

'But Slater didn't know!' the girl objected, shaking her head. 'So how could he have been waiting to waylay the shipment?'

'That's a good question.' Bill Dawson admitted. 'All I'm asking is, would you have any reason at all to think it *might* have been Slater or Noonan, one or the other, behind the leader's mask?'

She seemed to consider, and then she made a tired gesture. 'I don't know. I honestly don't. I was too worked up to notice anything, really. Except — Yes!' Her head lifted sharply at the memory. 'He had a quirt thonged to his wrist, I noticed particularly, because I remember I thought he was going to use it on me.'

'A quirt!' Bill Dawson nodded, grimly. 'As far as I'm concerned, that settles it!'

So they crippled into Renner, with a

contrived tandem hitch between the two wagons and a ten-horse team strung out ahead, and the bronc Bill Dawson had nearly ruined in his wild dash up the Loops trailing. Very little was said between the two people on the swaying wagon seat. Bill Dawson handled the horses; nervous exhaustion had taken the Trent girl and she leaned her head against the wagon bow and rode that way, eyes closed, the honey-coloured curls loose across her fine forehead as she swayed to the jolt of the springless vehicle. Bill observed her from time to time, thinking his own thoughts.

And thus, at last, he brought his teams into Tom McHail's farm yard; and as men came whooping and running from the farm house and barn the big wagons rolled to a stop.

8

The Big S ranch house was low and sprawling, fashioned — like the other headquarters buildings — of logs cut in the hills behind the ranch, with the bark left on. Together with the barn and bunkshack and corrals, it was a fitting backdrop for the crude and massive shape of the man who had built it, and who had laid his heavy, masterful hand over all the acres of North Renner.

Steve Slater waited at the top of the gallery steps, now, watching for the quartet of riders that came towards him through the stillness of late afternoon. A scowl warped his heavy features, narrowing his eyes, drawing down the brows and the corners of his mouth. The way those horsemen rode, one hunched over and swaying uncertainly in leather, told him all was not well here.

Their leader spurred ahead, finally, leaving the rest to come on at a pace adjusted to the hurt man's need. Pulling rein in front of the gallery, Virg Noonan returned Slater's glowering look; but the Big S boss hurled the first question before his ramrod had a chance to speak.

'Well, what went wrong?'

Noonan was in a poor mood. 'Everything!' he replied, hotly. 'A fine business you sent us into! Ed Wilcher's bad shot up, and losing more blood than is good for him. And we didn't manage the job we set out to do.'

'The hell you didn't!' Slater looked at the others who by now had reached the house, the bloody figure of Wilcher practically held upright in the saddle. 'Put him in his bunk,' he ordered, 'and let the cook see what can be done to stop him bleeding.' And, dismissing the wounded man with no more consideration than this, the Big S boss turned back to his foreman with a jerk of the head towards the door behind him.

'Come inside!' he grunted. 'We'll talk this out.'

He turned his back and walked into

153

the house not waiting for an answer. Noonan shrugged and swung from leather, dropping the reins to anchor the roan. Tramping up the split-log steps, he slapped his leg with the braided quirt which dangled as usual at his wrist. The other crewmen rode around the corner of the house, out of sight, with their hurt comrade.

The main room was a big one, that held a huge field-stone fireplace and massive, hand-hewn furniture. A gaping jawed bear rug, and sets of elk horns on each wall, spoke of Steve Slater's prowess with a long gun. Everything held the impress of the owner's masterful, dominating spirit, and showed the lack of any softening woman's touch.

As Noonan trailed his boss across the threshold, a man rose hastily from the leather-slung chair where he had been seated. The man was Tag Klebold; at sight of the scrawny, lantern-jawed figure a growl rumbled in big Noonan's throat. He strode directly across the room and, without preface, swung his hand in a

154

flat-palmed arc that cracked sharply as it struck Klebold's face.

The freighter, bleating in pain, was driven back into the chair. 'Get up!' cried Noonan, towering over him, blunt features dark with rage; his hands balled into craggy fists. 'Get on your feet and see what I do to you!'

Klebold was too frightened for speech. But Steve Slater's sharp voice stopped Noonan. 'Enough, Virg! What the hell's rowelling you?'

The man whirled on him. 'It was a trap! The skunk sent us after that seed wagon — and had one of his own men posted to ambush us.'

'It ain't true!' bleated Klebold. 'I dunno what you mean . . . '

'I suppose it wasn't that swamper of yours that busted in, to plug Wilcher and drive us off? I should of done more than horsewhip him, that day!'

The freighter's jaw dropped; his narrow face drained slowly of colour, until the imprint of Noonan's hand showed starkly against the pallor of his cheek.

'No!' he cried hoarsely. 'I don't believe it! I ordered Dawson to bring up a load of machinery! How could I have supposed he would — '

'Dawson?' Slater repeated the name. 'You don't mean that fellow who made trouble in the saloon? You gave him a job?'

'I'll can him again!' Klebold promised, in a weak fury. 'That damned meddler — interfering in something that didn't concern him.'

Slater turned on his foreman. He demanded ominously, 'Did you let anyone see you, coming up through South Renner?'

'Hell, I got better sense than that! We kept close to the timber.' Noonan shrugged thick shoulders. 'But now what? This thing has been a fiasco from the beginning. In the first place, it was the Trent girl driving the wagon. We hadn't figured on *that* and she may even have recognised some of us! Anyway, they got this load of seed through and now that we've tipped our hands, the next ones will be so well guarded we won't have a chance of stopping them.'

He turned and put his moody stare through a window, slapping his thigh furiously with the quirt.

'There won't be any next ones,' Steve Slater told him. 'I'll stop them — as I could have stopped this, if I'd known in time. The Trents can't get away with bucking me! Still, even one wagonload getting through to McHail's crowd can do a lot of damage.'

Tag Klebold had regained some of his colour, and gathered courage to put in a word of his own.

'Well, I tried,' he said, his voice holding the trace of a whine. 'You got to admit I tried. I passed the word along to you — and that, in spite of all the trouble you've made me in the past. I done you a real favour, Slater. I hope you ain't forgetting.'

The Big S boss flicked him a look weighted with contempt. 'You come here with your hat in your hand, you mean . . . selling out McHail in return for a deal with me. Well, my deals don't come cheap, d'you understand? And I don't make them with anybody that can't give me what I want in return!'

'But — '

'But what? Likely this business today has cost me one of my best riders, and it was the drifter you hired put the bullet in him. Without you do better than that, I got nothing for you!' Slater ended with a jerk of his head towards the door. 'Why don't you run along?'

Klebold came struggling up out of the depths of the chair, mouthing protests that died before they left his tongue. He looked at Slater; cast a wild look at Virg Noonan who did not even turn from his stand at the window. He made a last try: 'If you only realized the risk I took.'

'Beat it!' snapped the rancher.

And Tag Klebold obeyed, seething in fury but swallowing his helpless rage.

The spotted grey waited for him at a hitch pole in the ranch yard. He jerked up the cinches, with hands that trembled; piled into the saddle and rode away from

Big S in a state of emotional turmoil that had his teeth grinding painfully, and tears of frustration stinging his hollowed eyes. Gradually this storm subsided, and left him at the end of the short road that tied into the main wagon trace threading Renner Valley, north and south.

Here he drew rein, hesitating, at sudden loose ends. Sunset was a golden promise across the wide sky, firing up the clouds that floated on the piney crests to westward. He could spend the night in Renner City, but he had no business there; so he decided instead that he would push southward again, and put up at the McHails'. It would be a chance to find out what the sodbusters had to say about this day's doing.

That he would be breaking bread and taking lodging with people whom he had betrayed was not a matter to carry much weight with Tag Klebold . . .

Grey dusk was filtering like smoke through the last of daylight when he rode into South Renner. Not far from the McHail place he came across Frank

Harris, riding homeward, and the farmer gave him a warm greeting. 'We got our seed!' Harris cried, slapping a bulky sack that was strapped down behind his saddle. 'The Trents kept their word — the first wagon came up today and there'll be more to follow.'

'That's fine,' said Klebold, with a pleasure that he didn't make sound entirely wholehearted. 'Fine!'

'The damned Big S crew tried to stop delivery — they was masked, but it couldn't have been anybody else. And they'd have managed if it wasn't for this new driver of yours. He's a good man, Tag. Us Renner people owe you a lot of gratitude for bringing him in here.'

Klebold muttered something and rode on, in a dark mood. Gratitude, from the farmers; a booting in the teeth, from Steve Slater! This was all the coming of Bill Dawson had earned him so far — and not a dime of revenue from any source.

In fact, with his stupid interfering Dawson had managed to reconcile Trent and the farmers, and afterwards ruin the carefully figured scheme by which Klebold had figured to salvage something and make a new alignment with Big S.

All in all, Tag was feeling pretty badly abused as he rode in on the lamplit buildings of the McHail farm; and his darkest thoughts were centred on the man who called himself by the name of Dawson . . .

The McHail yard was alive with activity; lanterns had been lighted and the greybearded farm leader was tallying sacks of grain against a bill of lading, as his helpers finished tossing out the last of the load. Klebold reined up a minute to watch this work, glumly, and to return the friendly nod of greeting old McHail threw him.

Riding on to the barn then he off-saddled, found a stall for the spotted grey, and forked hay and a few ears of corn into the manger. He was turning away when he saw Bill Dawson leaning against an upright, silently watching him.

For some unclear reason, Klebold gave

a momentary start. He hadn't heard the young man come into the barn. He felt the probing of the other's cool glance and was strangely at a loss for words; but Dawson saved the moment by speaking himself.

'I brought your machinery up. It's in the wagon; and the horses are staked out for the night. One's a little the worse for wear, but he'll be all right. You can take a look if you want.'

Klebold said, gruffly, 'I'll take your word for it.'

Dawson pushed away from the upright. 'Going up to the house?'

They walked across the yard, a silent and oddly assorted pair. There was something reserved in Dawson's manner, the freighter couldn't help but notice. In an unexplained way, it made Klebold uneasy.

Bill Dawson let the other man enter the kitchen ahead of him. Inside, they found a trio of womenfolk: Mrs. McHail and her daughter, young Burke's wife; and Lila Trent. The two farm women were busy at stove and sink, finishing up a big meal for the men at work in the yard. Lila, tired from her trip and from her experience on the Loops, sat resting on one of the benches by the long table.

They all were talking in the liveliest manner; but when Lila glanced up at the noise of the screen door, her speech dropped off unfinished. The other two looked around; Mrs. McHail started a greeting but when she noticed the Trent girl's silence it did not quite come out.

In a sudden stillness, Klebold walked into the room with Dawson at his heels.

Bill halted near the door, watching the exchange of looks between these two business rivals. Klebold had removed his hat. 'Miss Trent,' he said, bobbing his head briefly. 'I heard there was some trouble. I'm glad it didn't come nothing.'

'I'm sure you are,' she said. 'Thank you.' But her voice sounded more as though he had paid her an insult. Klebold scowled, flicked a look around at the others.

'Mighty glad,' he repeated, in a lame

voice. And turned to snag his hat on a nail beside the door.

'Glad too, no doubt,' Lila added bitterly, 'that nothin happened to that machinery consignment for the Silver Queen.'

Klebold's lifted arm halted in midair; he stood this way during a long tick of the clock; then he turned his head and his sharp glance speared Bill Dawson.

'What did you tell — ?' The question broke off unfinished, as he read the firm assurance in Bill's stern look that the latter had not betrayed his secret knowledge of the kickback. Klebold shrugged thin shoulders, then, deliberately finished spearing his hat upon the nail.

Coming around, he faced the girl with palms lifted in a gesture. 'In business,' he said, 'a man gets along the best he can ...picks up an account when it's available and looking for a switch.'

'There was never the slightest complaint from the Silver Queen,' Lila rapped back at him. 'To take that account from us, you must have — ' She stopped, her pretty face suddenly colouring; it must have struck her all at once that she was very near to a cheap quarrel with this man, in the presence of others, and the thought had filled her with humiliation.

Suddenly she got to her feet and hurried from the kitchen into the other part of the house. Jean Burke exchanged a swift look with her mother, and hurried after her. Their going left an awkward silence.

Mrs. McHail broke this, saying, 'The poor girl has had a hard experience today ... Can I dish you men up some grub?' she went on, the subject abruptly changed. 'It's ready, and the rest will be in directly.'

'That would be right fine, ma'am,' agreed Bill Dawson, moving forward. 'I been smelling those hamhocks, and I don't need to be asked twice.'

And so the matter was passed over; but when Lila Trent returned later to the kitchen, which had filled now with the excited, high-spirited farmers fresh from the unloading of their wheat, it could be noticed that she kept a cool distance from Tag Klebold, and never again spoke to him during the course of the evening.

Tag noticed, certainly; but it made little impression on him, after the first bad moment of fear that Bill Dawson might have betrayed the guilty secret of his dealings with the Silver Queen manager. Tag Klebold wished mightily now that he had kept his mouth shut on that subject. He was beginning to wish more and more that he had never set eyes on this fiddle-footed stranger . . . especially when, shooting an occasional sly glance in his direction, he more than once found Bill Dawson watching him with a cryptic, thoughtful look, as though there were something about Klebold that he was bent on studying out. This ate at the man, bothering him.

At length the evening broke up, and these farmers of South Renner left for their homes and families, full of the plans that had been made for planting the new wheat. The Burkes were the last to leave, and before they did Tom Burke made Lila Trent a promise: 'Let us know when you're starting those other wagon loads up, and we'll be there in a body to help bring them through. Big S won't try that stuff again, I'm thinking!'

'Thank you,' said Lila Trent. But her smile was tired and her voice did not carry much hope. It was plain that worries for the future were resting upon her hard, tonight.

Shortly afterward, she excused herself and went to her room. She had been given the old room of Jean's for the night, and the McHail's regretted to tell their other guests that this left nothing better than the barn loft for them. Bill Dawson protested that, as tired as he was, the best room in a Denver hotel couldn't have sounded any better; Klebold mumbled something similar. So Tom McHail dug up and lighted an extra lantern for them.

'I'll take another look at the stock, before I turn in,' Bill Dawson told his boss shortly, when they were alone in the yard, behind the house.

'Guess I'll come along.'

They went out to the wagon and the picketed horses, the lantern in Tag Klebold's bony hand shuttling their shadows in long scissoring movements across the dark ground. They made their inspection in silence, finding all in order. They returned to the barn, then, and climbed the ladder to the rustling, clean-smelling hay.

Bill Dawson chose the spot he wanted. He took off his hat and scaled it to one side, yanked at the end of his gunbelt to free the buckle; but suddenly he hesitated, and then with a deliberate motion fastened the belt again. As he stood motionless, something pulled Klebold's glance to him. Seated in the hay, Klebold had one boot yanked off. He froze, meeting Dawson's stare in the glow of the lantern hanging from a nail.

Klebold's control suddenly gave way. 'Just who the hell,' he demanded, 'do you think you been staring at all evening?'

'I dunno,' said Dawson, 'but I got a notion it's the skunk who sicced Big S on that wheat wagon.'

The cold, spaced tones brought the other man scrambling to his feet, in one boot and one sock. Scrawny shoulders hunched, lantern jaw shot forward, Klebold staked his defence on bluster. 'You can't talk to me like that, you cheap drifter!'

'It figures,' Dawson went on, ignoring him and seeming to work out his thoughts as he went along — thoughts that had been bothering him and demanding clarification in precise speech. 'You had lost your chance of cutting the Trents out with them, so these farmers were no further use to you. Slater, on the other hand, might pay off for the tip that would keep that seed from getting here. It's plain somebody tipped him off — and it narrows down to you making that rush trip up here this morning; hiring me back in a hurry to fetch this machinery in to the mine, because you just couldn't wait to do it yourself — '

A squawl of fury broke from Klebold, and he was pawing at the pocket of his mackinaw. Dawson, not bothering to touch his holstered gun, simply took two strides and struck the other across the face with the back of his open hand, knocking him into the straw. He batted Klebold's arm aside and, reaching into the pocket himself, got the gun from it. He held this, looking at it and at the man grovelling in the piled straw at his feet.

'Honest,' he exclaimed, 'I dunno why I don't just go ahead and kill you and put you out of your misery . . . '

Anger had changed him, taken from him some of the deceptive, easy manner that had led Klebold to misjudge how far he could go with this fiddle-foot. Suddenly, Klebold was scared — scared of what he read in the other's hardened glance. The freighter heard his own voice babbling in a plea for mercy.

'Don't!' he cried. 'Please don't! Maybe — maybe I did say something to Slater . . . pass along the word that the Trents were going against his orders. A man's got to promote his own chances when he can, ain't he? But . . . I never dreamed he'd send Noonan and the crew to stop the wagon. Honest I never! You should have heard me when I found out — I really told the man where to get off.'

His voice was considerably steadier, by now; he had improvised so convincingly that he almost believed what he said, himself. Bill Dawson, though, did not appear convinced. Eyes shadowed under lowered brows, he continued to stare at Klebold; and the latter began to feel put upon at this scepticism.

'You don't think I'm telling the truth?'

'Not a word,' said Bill Dawson. 'Except that you betrayed the Trents and the farmers to Slater — *that* much, I can swallow.' But he shoved the captured six-gun into the pocket of his own leather jacket, ending the immediate threat of danger.

'I think I'll hang onto this until morning,' he grunted. 'I wouldn't sleep too well, knowing you had it back. Tomorrow you can hitch up your own damned teams and haul your own freight up to that crook at the mine. Me, I'm through with such ways of doing business; I figure to have no more of them. I quit! And this time I won't be hiring on again.'

'And good riddance!' snarled Klebold, defiant now that the gun was out of sight. 'Nor do you need think I'll pay you a penny for the meddling you've done.'

'Money you'd handled would leave a bad smell on my fingers; so, that's all right with me.' Bill Dawson turned away, then, with a jerk of his head at the lantern. 'Any time you're ready to blow that out is all right with me, too. I've had enough for one day. I'm turnin' in.'

He went back to the place he had already chosen for himself, and curled up comfortably in the hay. Almost instantly he was snoring.

Klebold sat where he was for a long moment, glaring at the sleeping man. Dawson seemed to have dismissed all thought of him; but the freighter noticed that he had left his gunbelt on and that his hand, as he slept, rested on the holster. Nor was there any possibility of getting the other gun from Dawson's jacket pocket.

Tag Klebold was not one to have tried such a maneuver, anyway. He took out his hatred in silent, furious seething. Then, pulling off the second boot, he rose and blew out the lantern, and returned to his bed in the hay. It was some time, though, before he could actually manage sleep.

9

It was early when Bill Dawson woke; despite the warmth generated by his own body and by the hay into which he had deeply burrowed, there was a chill from the night that helped to break through his slumber and rouse him. He lay for some moments before the seeping of dawn light through the loft told him where he was and brought the swift-moving current of events up to the present moment in time.

Stirring, then, he looked across at Tag Klebold. The freighter lay on his back, gaunt chest rising and falling, mouth open in a buzzing snore. He looked even less attractive in sleep than he did awake.

Bill Dawson thought, at least I'm through with that — for good! He had been on and off the Klebold payroll, in the past few days; but he knew now it was better to be out of a job entirely than to be attached to this ruthless man, by any strings. Unemployment was a familiar status. Working for such small-fry crookedness, not.

He got to his feet, stretching chilled limbs, and rasped a fist across beard stubble. Nearby, light seeped in through the partly-opened hay door. Bill walked over there in his sock feet, pushed the door wide and looked out upon the morning.

The last colours of sunrise still touched the sky; the new-risen sun gilded the piney rims and the cottony string of cloud that twined about Renner Peak's glistening flanks. Below, smoke pencilled from the kitchen chimney of the McHail farm house. And, leaning farther out, he saw a small figure in denims working around the emptied seed wagon and putting the freight teams into harness.

Quickly, Bill Dawson finished dressing by shoving into his flat-heeled boots and pulling on his hat. After that he was hurrying down the loft ladder and through the silent barn; and Lila Trent greeted him with a smile as he came to her across the morning's sparkling dew.

'Lemme help you,' said Bill, taking the harness. 'You're off to an early start, aren't you?'

'There's lots to do.' She looked fresh and pretty, he thought; the wan tiredness had vanished overnight and the bloom of warm, youthful colour in her cheeks seemed to brighten her eyes. The smile of thanks she gave Bill, as he took over the work of putting the freight teams on the chain, made him acutely conscious of his unkempt appearance beard stubble, and slept-in clothing. He regretted suddenly that this was to be the way she would remember him.

Because he wanted her to know, he said when the work was finished and the wagon was ready to roll: 'I quit Klebold. I don't like his methods. He can find other skinners who don't mind what kind of boss they work for.'

'And what will you do, Bill?'

There was interest behind her question, but he had no more adequate answer than a shrug. 'Drift, I suppose. The next job . . . the next rainbow. I always catch on somewhere.'

'I hope so, Bill!' She thrust out her hand suddenly, and he pulled off his hat as he took it, knowing this was goodbye. 'I hope you find the really big job — the one you deserve. And please remember: I . . . we . . . will always be grateful.'

'Thank you, ma'am,' said Bill.

A moment later he had handed her up to the high seat of the wagon. He helped her start the horses, yelling at them and scooping up a fistful of stones to chuck after them. He stood still, there in the meadow mists, and watched her turn the string in a wide arc and get them lined out upon the wagon road, southward. At the last, she leaned back and he saw her wave and swung his hat once in reply. Then she was gone.

He felt suddenly very lonely. He looked at the last stone that he still held; tossed it in his palm, and flung it away. He turned and went slowly over towards the house.

In the kitchen, he procured a basin of hot water from Mrs. McHail and did his shaving on the back stoop, in the thin chill of morning. He ran a comb through the cowlicks in his drab brown hair, without affecting much the lie of it. Afterwards, on the trestle table, he found crisp fried eggs and bacon, and buckwheat cakes dripping yellow butter. He was tying into a generous helping of this when Tag Klebold entered.

Klebold showed a cut on one sallow cheek, where Dawson's sharp blow the night before had broken the flesh deep. The two men did not speak, or look at one another. Klebold mumbled something at Mrs. McHail's cheery greeting and, shuflling around to a place at the far end of the table from where Dawson was sitting, dished up grub for himself. Having wolfed it down, he left without speaking half a dozen words.

There was activity in the yard when Bill Dawson stepped outside again. The Burkes had arrived, on the seat of their farm wagon, and old McHail was hitching up his own rig. Not many of the Renner Valley people had rolling stock, of any kind, and so it had been arranged for the few wagons that were available to distribute the bags of seed evenly among the homesteaders, enabling each man to get to work at once putting it into the ground while waiting for subsequent deliveries from Fair Play.

Dave Burke waved his good arm to Bill, who returned the greeting and touched hatbrim to Jean. Afterwards, Dawson went across to the barn. Out on the meadow, he saw Klebold fighting his teams into place on the chain, getting ready to roll up to the Silver Queen with his load of machinery. Klebold looked to be in a bad mood, and taking it out on the horses.

Bill walked into the barn and started putting gear on Klebold's spotted grey saddler. He was yanking up the cinches when the freighter entered. Klebold stopped short, scowling blackly.

'What the hell do you think you're doing?'

The younger man methodically knotted latigo into cinch ring, smoothed down the stirrup leather. 'I'm borrowing the grey,' he said. 'I have to have some way to get back down to Fair Play. I'll leave him in the stable there.'

'You'll leave him here!' snapped Klebold, the bony points of his cheeks colouring. 'You can walk back. Why didn't you hitch a ride with your lady friend?'

Dawson elected to ignore that cheap remark. He said coldly, 'There's a chore that's got to be done, here in the valley; I need the grey for it. Don't worry. It'll be in the stable waiting for you, all right; and the gun I took off you will be in the saddle pocket. I'm not asking, Klebold; I'm telling you!'

The look that paired this flat statement had a flinty edge to it, and something in its quality stilled Klebold's arguments. He had tested this fiddle-foot's mettle before, and apparently he felt no urge to try the experiment again. The corner of his thin mouth quirked a time or two; abruptly, Klebold heeled about and strode out of the barn.

Dawson watched him go. He took the

grey's bridle, then, to lead the animal from its stall. And halted as he caught sight of Jean Burke, in the shadows, her eyes pinned upon him in a face that looked pale against the gloom.

'I didn't intend to listen, but I couldn't help hearing.' Her voice was startled, breathless. 'You told Klebold there was a chore that had to be done. You — you were thinking of Virg Noonan, weren't you?'

'Noonan?' He wondered at the precise accuracy of her guess.

'He quirted you, and led the men that tried to kill Lila Trent. No, I don't think I'm wrong. I think you couldn't leave this country without a settlement.'

Bill acknowledged the point, with a brief shrug. 'All right. So I'm going after Noonan. It's a grudge — a personal matter. He added, bluntly, 'Do you figure to raise an objection?'

'Only that it's wrong to throw yourself away. Because that's what it would mean. Perhaps you could best Noonan; but Slater's men would kill you. What good is it to waste your life, in that manner?'

'I can look out for myself. Besides, I reckon it hardly matters much to anybody else what happens, since it don't to me.'

'But it does matter! It matters to your friends — '

'Just which friends?' His words were sharp, with an edge of bitterness.

'Why — all of us, here in the valley. Surely, you don't think that we can ever forget what you have done for us? You're a lonely person, I know . . . but no man is completely alone, and without anyone to wish him well. I'm sure if you ever took the time to double back, you'd find you had left a whole trail of potential friends behind you. Surely you must know that.'

Dawson thought it over, ready to deny it. He was feeling a little sorry for himself this morning, a little regretful of his rootless existence since saying goodbye to Lila Trent. He knew there was wisdom, and truth, in what this girl was saying; and yet he could not quite bring himself to agree.

'It ain't likely many people would give more than one thought to a drifter!'

'What you have to do, Bill Dawson,' she said, shaking her head a little, 'is to find the place you belong — the thing you're needed for.'

'I know what I'm needed for: to settle with the man who tried to run Lila Trent's wagon off the Loops!'

'And what good will it be to her, or Jabez, to have you dead, trying it? Alive, there's so many ways you could serve them.'

'I'd like to go to work for the Trents, but they can't afford to hire another man . . .' Bill Dawson blinked, suddenly jarred into a thought that had somehow not occurred to him before. All his life he had fought, in a highly competitive labour market, to get the pay he deserved for the work he did. Still, a dead man's hire would not come steep; and all at once he knew Jean was right — he would likely be a dead man if he went after Virg Noonan, and it would be a waste. So, instead, if he really wanted to do something for Lila Trent and her invalid father ...

'I'm a danged fool,' he blurted. 'And a blind one.' He grabbed the girl's arm, squeezed it. 'Thanks! Thanks for showing me sense.'

And, all at once eager to be riding, he turned away without further explanation and lifted into saddle. He grinned at Jean Burke, touching a finger to the brim of his shapeless hat. A moment later he had spurred out of the barn, out of the yard; had put his borrowed pony onto the southward trail leading out of the valley, and out of the hills.

He held the grey to a pretty steady pace, but Lila Trent had a long lead on him and it was not many hours short of Fair Play that he finally caught up with her. She had stopped to rest the teams; he had been watching for a dust stain hanging against the bright spring sky and the silver sage, and instead was almost upon the high-arched wagon and the horses before he saw it, drawn up beside the road.

Something leaped high in him and made him kick the horse eagerly ahead. He had his reward when the small, denimed figure of the girl came into view around the side of the wagon, one arm lifted to shade her eyes against the sun as she looked to see who it was approaching.

'Hi, stranger! 'she greeted him, then, her lips curving in recognition. Bill hauled the grey in and as the hoof-spurted dust settled he shoved his hat back from his forehead with the knuckle of a thumb, grinned down.

But all he could think of to say was, 'Hello!'

'I didn't know I'd be seeing you so soon,' Lila commented. 'You look like you're in a hurry to get somewhere.'

'Not too big a hurry. I could light awhile and breath my bronc, if I was asked.'

'You're asked.' She regarded the sweat-streaked horse as Bill swung to earth, let slack into the cinches, gave the heavy saddle a shake to ease it on the grey's back. 'That's Tag Klebold's grey,' she remarked then, her tone grown suddenly a little distant.

He answered the unspoken question. 'I borrowed him. My own sorrel is down in Fair Play. I told Tag I'd leave the grey there.'

'Then you've actually quit him?' The sun came out in her face again. 'I'm glad to hear it; I don't think you'd have been happy working for him.'

'I know danged well I wouldn't.'

Lila went on, 'I've got some grub Mrs. McHail put up for me. I don't know what capacity she imagined I had. Could you help me get rid of it?'

'Could I!' He let her lead the way around into the shade, where the lunch was spread. There, seated on the sandy ground with the branches of a lone pine murmuring overhead, they ate and washed down the food with cold tea. It was, to Bill Dawson, one of the pleasantest half-hours he could remember ever spending.

Through eating, he thanked her again

for sharing with him and fished up tobacco and paper. Carefully intent on what his hands were doing, he broached the subject that was uppermost in his thoughts.

'I want to talk to you and your father. I'd like to go to work for you.'

'For us?' He glanced at her and saw her puzzled frown, as she shook her head a little. 'Why, we'd like to give you a job, Bill . . . I'd have offered you one when I learned you had left Klebold. But — we just can't afford to hire a man now. I thought you understood that we couldn't, after our trouble with Slater. We've got to retrench, instead.'

'Sure, I understood all right. Still, I think maybe we could make a deal. I wouldn't cost you a lot: my eats, and four bits a week smoking tobacco. Room rent wouldn't come to anything at all; I've had a lot of experience sleeping in haylofts'

'I — I don't understand!' exclaimed Lila Trent. 'Why should you want to work for nothing, when you know you could draw top wages anywhere?'

Before answering, Bill Dawson stuck the cigarette between his lips, thumb-nailed a match to life and shaded it with his palms as he got the smoke burning. Throwing aside the match, he said:

'You probably think I'm crazy, all right. I wouldn't argue the point. But what do I want with money? That's all I've ever worked for, and there was never any fun in it. Maybe that's why I've been such a danged fiddle-foot, getting bored with one place and moving on — looking for a prettier rainbow over the next hill. And never finding it.

'Well, here for the first time I've found reason for wanting to stick around. Hard to put into words just what it might be: people that I'd like a chance to know a little better, maybe. Or maybe somebody to get good and mad at.'

She waited, her grey eyes on him, a serious expression in her face. She had had the good sense not to interrupt his talking, guessing, perhaps, that he was thinking things out, aloud, and that what he said was for his own benefit as much as hers. Now, however, she prompted him as he halted: 'You're mad at somebody?'

'Boiling mad! I might think this whole affair was none of my business, but I've got the mark of a quirt, and the memory of bullets flying around my head yesterday on the Loops, to remind me that it is. Somehow, after what's happened, I just wouldn't feel right to move on without waiting to see that range-hog Big S outfit taken down a peg; and this seems to be the logical place for me to grab a hold in the fight.

'So how about it? Will you hire me, on those terms?'

He waited for her answer, quietly working at the butt he had fashioned. Lila Trent had lowered her eyes to the hands knotted in her lap, and Bill studied her, unnoticed — the curve of her cheek, the way the ends of her honey-golden hair curled crisply against her throat. There was no sound for awhile, other than the murmur of the pine branches overhead.

The girl lifted her head, then, and her

grey eyes met his own, levelly. 'No,' she told him, firmly. 'Not on those terms. We could never take such advantage of your generosity.'

Bill Dawson's mouth pulled down. He shrugged, stubbed his cigarette in the dirt, reached for the hat he had laid aside. 'Well, that's that, I guess. But I'm plumb disappointed.'

She wasn't quite finished. 'There's only one condition on which I'd consider making a deal; as for my father, he'll have to answer in his own name. We can't pay you a decent wage — now — but if we win our fight, some day we may again, I'd insist on keeping a tab and, when that day came, making a settlement of what we owed you by then.'

Bill's mouth widened slowly into a grin. 'You had me scared for a minute, Miss Trent! Your conditions are such as I'd be glad to accept. It's a deal then?'

'We'll talk to Dad. I still think we'd be taking an awful advantage.'

'If I'm too dumb to know the difference, then keep quiet about it and maybe I won't catch on.' Bill Dawson came lightly to his feet, offered the girl a hand to help her up. 'We might as well be getting this outfit back on the road.'

She kept his hand for a moment longer than she needed; her smile was warm, her eyes sparkling. 'I do thank you, Bill Dawson!' she exclaimed, with quiet sincerity. 'We're in desperate circumstances, and you know it. What you've just offered could mean the saving of us.'

'I dunno about that,' he said, embarrassed, but deeply touched by her words and tingling to her small palm within his own. 'But we'll sure enough give 'em a fight . . . '

★ ★ ★

That evening, at a conference in old Jabez Trent's sick room, the agreement was confirmed. Jabez seemed at first as reluctant as his daughter had been to accept Dawson's proposition, but when the young man's attitude was made clear.

he agreed — though with a reiteration of Lila's heartfelt thanks.

'If your aim is to clip Steve Slater's horns for him,' he admitted, 'then helping this freight line to stay in business is one way of doing it. We've thrown in our lot with the South Renner people, come what may. And they're going to need our support if they're to hold out against him. After that doings on the Loops, yesterday, it's clear the issues are drawn.'

'Slater will never give us that extension, now,' Lila Trent said. 'There's no point even asking him.'

Bill Dawson agreed, drily. 'Not if he'd send his men to wreck the wagon and kill you. Any friend of the South Renner farmers is off his books. It used to be Tag Klebold; now, apparently, you and Tag are going to be tradin places.'

Old Trent's seamed face clouded, as he considered this. 'Klebold — and Slater! That would be a tough combination to buck.'

'You might as well get used to the idea. They're two of a kind — mean and unscrupulous. Klebold went to Slater with the word that you were sending up that wheat, contrary to his orders; it was a bid for Slater's support and undoubtedly he'll get it, because of course Big S needs some kind of a freight line operating. And, being a vindictive sort of gent, I fully expect to see Slater backing Klebold to the hilt, so as to help crowd you off the trails and point a warning to anyone else that dares to cross him.'

A sober silence greeted this warning. It was so still that Bill Dawson could hear the ticking of a clock in the hall outside the sickroom.

Lila Trent said then, in a small voice, 'If it comes to that, I suppose then we're beaten before we begin.'

'Not at all!' said Bill, firmly. 'It just means we got a fight on our hands — a fight for survival, that bears on the future of the South Renner people as well as that of the freight line. We can count on seeing dirty fighting, too, with every trick that men like Slater and Klebold are able to think of. But sabotage and violence are weapons both sides can use . . . ' Jabez Trent lifted a pallid, deep-veined hand in protest.

'No!' he cried. 'Fair Play'' has been the name of my company; and it's been my motto, all through the years. I'll fight clean, or not at all. I want that understood.'

'All right.' Bill Dawson hitched to his feet; walked to the window for a brief look into the night, turned back again. 'A fair fight, then — against Klebold and Slater's brand of crookedness. All I can say is that I wish us luck. And the first job,' he added, 'is to meet the note that falls due the first of the month.'

'That has to be done,' Lila said. 'It's going to take some hard figuring, especially with the loss of the Silver Queen account. Tomorrow morning we'll go over the books and see how it's to be managed.'

Bill Dawson was weary enough, and Lila Trent's face held tiredness. Nevertheless he told her, 'It's early, and time's short. I don't think that had better wait until morning.'

Jabez Trent nodded his gaunt, white-thatched head. 'The boy's right. Fetch the books, girl. Fetch them and we'll start laying our war plans — right now . . .'

10

That was the beginning; and in the days that followed, Bill Dawson often found himself wondering where it all would end. The further he got into this job, the more hopeless it looked . . . and the greater determination he had to see it through. The Trents, for their part, proved more than ready to trust to his advice — seemed to depend, more and more, on whatever help he could give them.

A glance at the books had told him much. They were a record of the valiant fight Lila Trent had been putting up, almost singlehanded, during these hard and dragging months since her father's illness. She had fought bravely and had managed well, yet the requirements of old Jabez Trent's condition had drained the business steadily; and now, since the break with Slater, only the greatest of sacrifices could hope to pull them over the hump and meet the note payment so shortly to come due.

Further meetings in Jabez Trent's sick room laid down the lines on which this retrenchment must be made. Costs had to be shaved, in every department. Orders which Lila had recently placed for new wagons and equipment were cancelled; Bill, who was a natural-born mechanic and had had, among his many other occupations, considerable training as a wheelwright and carpenter, pointed out that some of the older rolling stock which normally was due for the scrap heap could, with considerable labour, be repaired and patched up enough for further use. Still others, he recommended, should be repainted and sold, for cash. The livestock, too, must be thinned out to cut feed bills, and the payroll reduced.

It meant, as old Jabez had predicted, cutting back to a point which the freight line had passed long ago — almost starting over. It meant discarding many accounts which, on this marginal basis, they could no longer afford to keep. It meant firing men who had been on the payroll for years, in order to save the money for their wages.

This involved no great hardship on most of the men concerned, for a reason that Bill Dawson grimly foresaw. On the day that the redheaded teamster, O'Shay, came into the office to draw his time, the Irishman told Lila, 'I'm sorry to be leavin' you; it's been a good outfit to work for. But a man's got to consider his own future, and I've already had an offer of another job.'

'Don't tell us!' grunted Bill, from the doorway. 'It's Tag Klebold.'

O'Shay looked embarrassed. 'Why, yeah. I got little use for him, myself. Still, it's a job. I never would have quit the Trents to go to work for a competitor — but after all, I been fired.'

'Of course,' Lila hastened to assure him. 'Nobody's blaming you ...' But later, when the man had gone, she asked Bill, 'Klebold is hiring hands? I didn't know.'

'It was just a guess. After all, this business we've been forced to turn down has to go to somebody — who but Tag? Like it or not, Klebold is on the other end of this seesaw: as we go down, he goes up.'

'Do you suppose Slater is backing him?'

'Not yet, maybe. I reckon Tag is doing all right without help — just picking up what we slough off. And naturally, expanding like that, he's in the market for more skinners, more yardhands. Maybe,' he added, on the impulse, 'he can use some of these wagons I'm fixing up for sale. Tag's a cheapskate — show him something that looks like a bargain and if you're smart you can likely steal him blind. Yeah, I'll have to see what I can do with him . . . '

Bill was doing work enough for three men . . . more work, for food and tobacco and a bed in the stock barn hayloft, than he had ever given for good pay. He personally went over every scrap of equipment, judging what could be salvaged for further use, and what could be sold for as much as it might bring. He pitched into the job of repairing and painting the big wagons; he toiled endlessly, tearing out faulty timbers and replacing them with new, sound lumber; by his labours he changed ancient outfits that had been ready for the junkheap into newly serviceable rigs with plenty of miles still in them.

Then he looked Klebold up and found the lantern-jawed freighter in his wagon yard. Klebold was strutting about importantly and hurling orders to a crew of workmen. There seemed to be real activity afoot, with carpenters ripping weathered shingles off the crazy, swaybacked barn, to make way for new support timbers and a new roof. Painters were at work freshening up the sun-blistered, rain-streaked paint job on the office building. A bigger and more expensive sign was going up over the wagon yard entrance.

Klebold had changed, too. He'd discarded the old red mackinaw and bought himself a new outfit — tweed coat and breeches, and high boots polished to such a shine that highlights twinkled up and down the leather at every step he took. Bill Dawson suspected that the new clothes had been modelled after Steve Slater's expensive garb, but Klebold didn't have the frame to wear them properly. They hung unbecomingly on the man's gaunt bones, making him look skinnier and more unprepossessing than ever.

Bill Dawson said drily, 'Come up in the world since last I seen you, Tag!'

The freighter, busy with his orders to the workmen, hadn't heard his approach and he whirled around as though stung; fear flickered in his hollow eyes and anger at once replaced this, as he got hasty control of himself. Obviously he was remembering that last encounter with Bill Dawson, and the clout in the face it had led to.

'What do you want?' he demanded, with harsh suspicion. One bony hand started sliding towards the tail of his unbuttoned coat, that half concealed a belt-slung holster.

Dawson eyed the hand and Klebold

flexed it and dropped it to his side, his sallow face colouring. A bleak, humourless grin quirked Bill's mouth.

'That's better,' he grunted. He had made no move himself, or taken his hands from where they rested with thumbs hooked into his jeans belt. He said, 'I hear you're taking on new men?'

'And I hear the Trents are lettin' 'em go!' A new thought kindled the other's sharp stare. 'It couldn't be you've got the gall to come to me lookin' for a job?'

'Nope — it couldn't!' snapped Bill. 'I like it where I am. I figure to stay awhile.'

'Just how long? You people ain't foolin' me, or anybody else. The skids are under them high and mighty Trents at last — and greased good. And I'm havin' the time of my life, watchin' 'em slide.'

'I could figure as much. Now, do you want to hear what I came to see you about? It's a business matter.'

Klebold's eyes narrowed a little. 'Keep talkin'.'

So Bill told about the wagons he had for sale. He had never done any selling before, varied as his career had been; but he proved now that he would have been an expert. His approach was exactly right — he talked poor, with just the correct degree of defiance, and it did not take him long to sense that he had his man on the hook. Klebold's small-souled instinct for hunting a bargain saw here what looked like a rare chance to get a beaten rival with his back to wall, and take advantage of him.

He was careful not to show too great an interest, though. When Bill had finished he shrugged his bony shoulders and said, disdainfully, 'Well, it might be worth a look. Maybe I'll drop around one of these days if I find a few minutes to spare.'

'We can't promise to hold them for you,' said Bill. His tone, and the plain reluctance with which he left the thing on this basis, conveyed that he had small hope of selling the wagons anywhere else, and that his employers were in desperate need for quick money from a sale.

He gave Klebold two days to make his

visit, but the man wasn't able to hold out longer than twenty-four hours: the fear of losing a bargain, and the pleasure of lording it over his rivals, overcame the desire to keep them on pins waiting for him. He came strolling into the Trent freight yard next day, twirling a walking stick that he had added to his newly-elegant ensemble, and with an air of vast superiority that made Lila Trent clench her fists as she watched him from the office window.

'Look at him!' she exclaimed tightly. 'That a man could be so small — '

Bill muttered, 'Keep out of sight. There's no need why you should have to take his bullying. I'll handle this bird!'

He stepped out and intercepted the visitor, quickly steering him away from the office towards a line of high-bowed wagons, freshly painted and gleaming, ranged along the fence.

Klebold looked them over with a critical eye, but Bill Dawson knew that the man's conviction of getting himself a bargain and at the same time humiliating the Trents probably had him blinded to the actual shape these vehicles were in; probably, too, he lacked appreciation of Bill Dawson's many talents. It would have taken more than the casual inspection Klebold gave them to tell that these wagons were actually some of the oldest and least serviceable that Bill had managed to rescue from the junk heap, and give a deceptive appearance of being only slightly used.

'What price do you want? 'Klebold demanded.

Bill named him one that was purposely high, and waited. He watched a carefully prepared look of scorn warp the man's arrogant features. 'Too much by five hundred dollars!' Klebold snapped.

The other tried to look unhappy. 'Split the difference?' he begged, as in a last resort.

'No! Take it or leave it — that's as far as I'll go!' Klebold twirled his walking stick, turned away. 'Think it over.'

'I — I reckon we'll take it!' agreed Bill Dawson, meekly. 'Miss Trent won't like this, but I'll try to convince her.'

Tag Klebold smirked. 'You try real hard. I'll have the money for you next week. I know damn well you'll be around for it!' And with this he took his strutting departure.

Behind his back, Bill Dawson grinned broadly. 'What you *don't* know,' he grunted, in deep satisfaction, 'is that you just made a deal for about three times what these broken down wrecks are worth. You were that anxious to cheat somebody out of something . . .'

He went into the office in a mood of high accomplishment, to tell Lila Trent the outcome of his dickering. He knew it would mean for her a very real lift to the spirits. Klebold's money would help a lot towards the nearing deadline at the first of the month.

In addition to his other chores, Bill Dawson was working nearly full time as a wagoneer, taking shipments out upon the freight trails when the diminished crew lacked men to spare for the job. He had to watch himself that he did not drive the horses mercilessly as he drove himself; a kind of fury seemed to have entered him — a need to press harder an harder, and impatience with the amount that he was able to accomplish.

Lila spoke of this, anxiously. 'You're killing yourself for us!' she insisted. 'We shouldn't let you do all you're doing — it's not right.'

'I'm not doing any more than I want to,' he assured her. 'Tell you the truth, I'm getting sort of a bang out of it — it's that much pleasure, showing a man like Slater that decent folks can exist without licking his boots and taking his dirty orders.'

'Then — you really think we've got a chance to whip this thing?'

Bill looked down at her, in the lamplight which glimmered faintly around them there on the porch of the big white house; she looked tired but very lovely, and her eyes were dark pools.

'Why not?' he grunted. 'No man's whipped while there's fight left in him. As long as you've got a wagon on the road, you're still in business.'

'But even if we manage, somehow, to get out of debt to Steve Slater, Dad and I are piling up another debt that we can hardly hope to pay. I'm thinking of what we owe you, Bill.'

Something in her voice, in the nearness of her, gave him the temerity to place a hand upon her arm. She did not draw away. They stood very close together, and her face was raised to his, and he thought her breast lifted on a quickly drawn breath.

But then he dropped his hand and stepped back, numb with sudden shame at the impulse that had throbbed through him. Lila Trent's gratitude was very real, and very deep; but he could not take advantage of it. He could not spoil their relationship in any such crude way as that.

He said, gruffly, 'You don't owe me anything — anything at all. Please try to remember!' And, pulling on his battered sodbuster, he added, 'I won't come in tonight. Tell your father hello for me. I'm leaving early for Renner City . . . '

Abruptly as that, he left her. He did not glance back and so did not see her standing there and looking after him, a troubled frown on her face, for long minutes after he had passed from sight down the avenue of trees that were just leafing out with the first green bursts of spring.

He had a mixed load to deliver in Renner City next day — grain for the livery stable, a consignment of leather goods for the town's saddle shop — as well as some rolls of barbed wire and boxes of nails to be dropped off en route for the farmers of South Renner. He found the nester places abuzz with activity. They had received the bulk of their wheat seed a few days before, and were working through every hour of daylight getting it into the waiting ground; the best planting time was already nearly spent, in the delay of having this seed released from the Trent warehouse.

He made his usual overnight stop at the McHail place, and the folks there were all glad to see him and anxious for news of the Trents. They knew of the slow, uphlll fight that was going on and, feeling a responsibility for the break between the Trents and Steve Slater, were deeply concerned over the problems that faced the beleaguered freight line.

Old Tom McHail, pulling at his white beard, scowled into the dusk beyond the kitchen window and said fervently, 'We got 'em into this fight and we only wish there was someway we could help. Especially, knowing how bad they need money right now and how deep we are into the books with not a cent to contribute. Come market season, if we can all hang on that long, us here in South Renner should have the cash to wipe out a lot of our indebtedness. But as of right now . . . '

'Right now,' Bill Dawson finished, 'you've got your own hands plenty full — and with Steve Slater, at that! You dig down to the bottom of every man's trouble, hereabouts, and you're likely to turn up something foul-smelling, that's tied up with that man and his money-power and his greed. But if we all keep fighting, maybe in the end we'll combine our strength and lick him.'

Mrs. McHail wanted to know, 'What about the note that's due?'

'We'll meet it,' said Bill. 'One way or another. Cash is low at the tail end of a hard winter season, but once we make this hurdle there'll be plenty of business to take us through the rest of the year. After that, we'll be counting pretty heavily on you.'

He added, 'So I hope you're keeping a close watch on the seed you've put in.'

'Why do you suppose we've ordered this extra wire?' McHail demanded. 'Don't worry — we won't be caught napping. We're reinforcing the boundary fence, across the valley's narrow waist. There's not going to be any cases of Slater's cattle breaking it down and getting into our wheat — by accident, or otherwise!'

Bill Dawson nodded grimly. 'That's a realistic way to look at it. As long as your eyes are that wide open, you should get along.'

Morning was as clear as it can only be in the high mountain valleys, with a sky of startling blue and with Renner Peak dazzlingly aglow in the risen sun. It made this a beautiful place indeed, and one that any man would have fought to keep.

Waking, of a morning, to look out at old Renner's frosty shape rising at your very doorstep . . . having its shadow touch you of an evening . . . seeing that majestic, unchanging eminence above the shifting mists, or with its timeless snowfields sparkling under the silent stars of winter: even a fiddle-foot could appreciate something of what this might mean to a man. In time, it seemed to Bill Dawson, some of its majesty would get into a man's soul and his soul would expand to fit it. And then no other spot on earth could seem so fair, again.

Yes, Bill Dawson admitted, there was much that he could learn from the men of Renner Valley.

As he rolled up the long, timber-walled

trough of the valley, he could see these men at work in their fields. Yonder, he watched one sowing the precious seed, scattering it broadcast with a long swing of his arm as he walked down the uneven furrows, the seed making a shimmer in the air about him where the sunlight touched it. A woman came to the door of a humble but homelike tarpaper building that stood close to the wagon road, and when she recognized him she waved and came hurrying out.

Dawson kicked the brake, halting his teams with a couple of jerks at the long line. He touched hatbrim to Jean Burke, in a respectful and friendly greeting.

'Glad to see you, ma'am,' he said. 'I been wanting an awful lot to thank you.'

'Thank me?' She stood with a hand upon a spoke of the big wheel, peering up as though uncertain of his meaning. 'For what?'

'For the most considerate favour any person ever took the trouble to do me . . . for stopping me from a dumb impulse, that morning, and showing me something better than running after a few more tarnished rainbows.'

'You are happy?'

He grinned. 'I'm working harder than I ever worked in my life, with likely nothing ahead but starvation if I keep it up much longer. Sure, I'm happy! Having more fun than I ever did.'

She saw the seriousness behind his banter and she smiled, nodding. 'I'm glad, Bill. I'm glad I guessed right.'

Bill asked after her health, and her husband's. Dave's arm, she told him, was much improved. He had had it out of the bandages for days now and there was only a little stiffness yet. Neighbours had helped with the work he couldn't do while he was laid up, and there had been no loss of time.

'That's fine,' said Dawson, and straightened on the seat. 'Well, I'd better be rolling. Haven't got all day to get up to Renner City and back.'

A shadow crossed her glance, and he knew what she was thinking. 'Don't worry. I'm not hunting Virgil Noonan, or Slater, either one. I'm a business man, now — got no time for personal feuding. You knocked *that* foolishness out of me, for good and all.'

'But — 'There was alarm in her faltering words. 'They might have a different idea. You're crossing Big S, alone . . . riding into Slater's stronghold. What if they want to make trouble?'

He touched the Eisley in its cutdown holster. 'I can make a little trouble myself, then, I reckon. Still, it's hardly likely I'll have to. Trying to pull rough stuff out on the Loops is something else again, from trying it in the valley itself. Anyway, there are people in that town who depend on wagon freight and I can't let a little thing like Slater and his tough crew scare me out of delivering.' He flashed his grin. 'But thanks for being concerned about me, ma'am. I promise to keep out of mischief!'

He knew, however, as the heavy wagon lumbered on, that anxiety still weighted the frown he left upon her face.

11

He was himself a long way from feeling quite as sure as he'd tried to sound. There was plenty of reason for thinking he could expect trouble with Big S if he encountered any of its crew. Slater and Noonan weren't apt to forgive the man who had broken up their play to wreck the wheat wagon, and wounded one of their riders into the bargain — and then boldly gone to work for the doomed Trent freight line. So Bill Dawson felt an unpleasant tightening of nerves as his teams strung out along the road to North Renner.

When presently he passed the bottleneck where the valley walls pinched together and four-strand wire bridged the gap marking Steve Slater's boundary, Dawson hitched his gun belt around so the scarred holster lay handy, across his legs; and he tried the gun, sliding it in and out of leather a time or two to make sure it wouldn't stick. He rode with a restless eye, after that, checking the rolling grass bottoms for any far glimpse of approaching horsemen. If there was to be trouble, he wanted warning of it.

Yet, the crossing of Big S range occurred without any mishap. He even stopped briefly for watering, at the point where had occurred the trouble with Noonan that day, and caught up the teams again and pushed on — still without raising sign of a Slater horseman. And so he came at last, with midafternoon, into sight of the sprawling tilt of Renner City's main street.

The muddy morass that the town had been, the day of his first arrival here, was pretty largely dried under the warmth of long, spring sunshine. The broad sea of slop between the double line of buildings and sidewalk plankings had turned into a fairly solid expanse chopped by deep hoof marks and rutted by wagon wheels. This was an improvement, but nothing could add real beauty to the dismal place.

Bill Dawson first set about discharging the freight he had hauled up with him, at the livery barn and the saddle shop and the other establishments which, together, had made up the wagonload with their separate orders. This took considerable time. Afterwards, he watered and grained his teams, readying for the return trip. As he was finishing this, a baldheaded man in shirt sleeves came towards him along the muddy planking, stood a moment watching the work.

When Dawson nodded greeting the man said, without other preface, 'I run the mercantile across the street. I need somebody to haul my stuff from railhead. Would the Trents take on my account?'

Bill Dawson frowned, puzzled. 'I understood Tag Klebold did your hauling for you?'

'Klebold!' The man made a face. 'Did you know, that guy threw me over? Told me all at once he had new accounts that were worth more to him and he wouldn't be hauling for me any longer. Left me stranded, damn him!'

The younger man frowned. He remembered how disdainfully Klebold had talked about the mercantile account; now that he was climbing in the world he thought he could afford to pick and choose his business, and lightly throw aside an old, established client.

'Feeling pretty sure of himself, isn't he?' he grunted.

'And what am I supposed to do?' the other protested. 'Go out of business? Looks like I'll have to, unless the Trents will take me on.'

'No need to worry.' Bill had done some quick mental computation. The mercantile account was not worth a great deal in terms of money — in fact, it could mean a loss except that the Trents' big wagons were able to load several such small consignments on a single trip. Still, there were the intangible values of good will, and of showing up Tag Klebold's dubious ethics; and it was an opportunity not to be missed.

'Sure,' Bill said. 'We'll take your business. If you got an order ready, I'll take it along with me now.'

The man thanked him heartily. 'Got the list right in my pocket,' he said, producing it. 'This saves my life. A man like Klebold that would leave a customer in the lurch — he don't deserve to stay in business.'

'I reckon you may have a point there,' Dawson agreed, taking the order. He was thinking that this sort of thing was bound to get around, sooner or later. And it showed the difference in the methods of Klebold and of those he was attempting to displace.

Bill was hungry by now, but he did not want to waste any more time than necessary since his business in this town was finished. A sandwich, that he could tote with him, would do. And maybe a quick beer — he could allow himself that much of relaxation.

So he entered the same eat shack where he'd dined the other time he was here. The sizzle and aroma of fry meat filled the air of the little place; a single customer was waiting while the sour-faced cook in the greasy apron got a steak and onions ready. As Bill stepped to the counter the cook threw him a look across one shoulder, telling him gruffly, 'Take a seat, buddy. I'll be with you in a minute.'

'I'm in a hurry,' Bill told him. 'Just throw some stuff into a sandwich for me. Anything you got — a slab of cold roast beef would be fine. Cut the bread thick and use plenty of pepper.'

The cook flopped his steak over, in a splutter of hot grease. 'I said, you'll have to wait your turn — ' Then he got his first careful look at the newcomer and recognized him.

'Hey! You're the man was in town last week; raised a row at the saloon with Slatcr and his whole crew!' This knowledge had raised a sudden respect in the man — maybe even a trace of fear. He hesitated; took another look at the meat in the pan, and made his decision.

'Yeah,' he grunted. 'I guess I can throw a sandwich together. You'll excuse me, Mr. Kimberly,' he added appealing to the other customer. 'This won't take but a minute, and your steak ain't quite done yet. . . .'

He hurried out to the icebox room. And Bill Dawson, turning, laid his stare fully on the man seated at the counter.

The name of Kimberly had struck a familiar chord; and now, looking at the man in the Eastern-cut sack suit, his clean-shaven features showing a pallor and softness unsuited to this climate of strong sunlight and harsh winds, Bill suddenly knew who he was and where he had seen the name before. He had seen it, written in a cramped and spiderish hand, across the bottom of a freighting contract drawn between Tag Klebold and the manager of the Silver Queen syndicate mine.

'So you're Kimberly,' Bill murmured, quietly. 'I was wondering what you'd be like.'

There was something supercilious in the curve of the Easterner's full lips, but his eyes were hooded and careful. 'I don't think,' he said, coldly, 'that I know you — or what you're talking about!'

'I think I could make it plain enough. The name is Dawson. I'm a teamster for Jabez Trent.'

'Yes?' The stare became edged with flint, more tightly careful than ever. But Kimberly said only, 'I used to do some business with him, if I'm not mistaken.'

'You're not mistaken. Your mistake was in quitting him for Tag Klebold — on the terms you did. That was a pretty raw error, friend.'

'Explain yourself!' The syndicate man's voice had turned clipped and harsh.

Dawson shrugged. 'Just mention my name to Klebold — ask him if he showed me the contract you signed with him . . . and then if he told me the unwritten agreement that went with it.

'It can be dangerous, tying yourself in a crooked deal with a cheap crook like Klebold, when you aren't sure that he knows how to keep his mouth shut. It would be too bad, now, wouldn't it, if word somehow leaked back to your bosses in the East that money the syndicate was paying for freight bills was finding its way back into your own pocket? Oh — here's my sandwich,' he broke off, 'finished already.'

The cook came waddling back into the room, with the paper-wrapped package. Bill nodded his thanks, tossing money onto the counter. 'Looks like the rains have stopped, don't it?' he commented mildly. 'Could be a spell of right pleasant weather ahead.'

He slipped the sandwich into a pocket, and left the eat shack. He did not look at the syndicate man again; he didn't have to. He had made his point, and it had taken its toll. He was very sure that Kimberly was not going to enjoy that particular dish of steak and onions.

In fact, Bill Dawson was pretty well pleased with himself. He had put fear into the syndicate man, and a very proper uneasiness over the kickback deal with Klebold. It might even prove enough to break Kimberly away from that contract and bring him back to Jabez Trent, as the price for keeping Dawson's mouth shut. Anyway, Bill figured he was doing a very good piece of work today of discrediting Klebold. Tag should start feeling the effects, before long.

Looking at it this way, Bill felt more than ever that he deserved the short beer he had promised himself; so he went the half block to the saloon, pausing en route toss his sandwich up onto the wagon seat. The town was utterly dead today, with no traffic at all through the tilted street or along the plank walk. One or two saddle horses stomped at hitch rails but that was all. The sodden echo of his own flatheeled boots along the wooden walk was about the only sound.

The saloon, too, was deserted except for a bored bartender dealing himself poker hands at onc of the tables. It was not the one who had been on duty that other time, and so he took no particular interest in this newcomer; he merely hitched to his feet and went around the counter for the beer that Dawson ordered, with no comment more expressive than a grunt as he scooped up the coin Bill threw down in payment. Bill took time to enjoy the beer, not eager to resign himself again to the hard jolting of a wagon seat.

He was still standing there when Big S came cavalcading into the quiet town.

It was just as on that other day. The steady drum of horses began swelling in the stillness, and then here they were, pouring up the muddy street — an arrogant tide of men on tough-jawed, shaggy range broncs. Bill set down his glass, and sleeved his mouth as he turned quickly to the door; but if he had any thought of flight it was already too late.

Even now they were hauling up in front of the saloon, piling out of saddle, anchoring their horses at the tooth-marked hitching rail. They tromped across the boardwalk plankings, crowding up as they shoved the glass doors open. When they came, laughing and loud-talking, across the threshold of the big, sour-smelling room, Virg Noonan and Steve Slater were in the van.

And Bill Dawson knew he was in for trouble.

Noonan saw him first, and the range boss stopped in his tracks so abruptly that the man at his back overran him. The impact scarcely jarred the solid weight of the big fellow, braced as he was on widely-planted boots, and it didn't deflect the stare he pinned on the solitary figure at the bar. 'Well, I'll be damned!' grunted Noonan.

Next moment, Slater and the rest had sighted the cause of his exclamation, and at once the loud talk was smothered. The last Big S cowhand had crowded in now, shutting the door with a rattle of the loose pane; there were six of them, besides their two bosses. And it was patent that Bill Dawson, facing them from the counter with the half-finished beer forgotten at his elbow, had no one at all.

Slater saw it, with a mean-eyed glance that flicked and probed into every corner of the dingy room before it came back to settle on Dawson. The edges of his mouth puckered upward, in a grin of wicked pleasure.

But he did not hurry this. With a sideward jerk of the head he threw an order at the bartender, who instantly set out a bottle and a pair of whiskey glasses. 'Get 'em,' Slater told his range boss; to the rest he said, 'Belly up, boys, and name your wishes. This one is on me.' Afterwards, while the crewmen started a quick stampede to the bar, he walked over to a table and eased into a barrel chair. Noonan hesitated, then went and got the bottle and glasses in his big hands and followed his chief to the table, where he twisted a chair about so that it faced Dawson. Slater had already run liquor into the glasses. They sat like that, Noonan with his braided quirt laid beside him, both holding their drinks and taking them slowly while they studied Bill Dawson with interest and silent amusement.

He knew they were playing a game with him, having plenty of time to finish whatever they had in mind. Friendless, he had no chance against so many if they wanted to take him.

But their cat-and-mouse attitude built

a sudden, stubborn defiance in him. Jaw muscles knotting, Bill Dawson turned and swept up his beer mug, finished down the warm brew and slapped the schooner onto the wood, empty. Then he walked deliberately forward, to the very table where Vir Noonan and Steve Slater were sitting. With every eye in that room pinned on him, he pulled back a chair for himself, uninvited, and dropped into it.

'So here we all are,' he murmured.

Big Noonan had half risen to his feet. 'Why, you damned punk . . . ' His voice was a coarse snarl, and the gold tooth glinted beneath his curling lip. 'You think you got time for jokes, do you?'

'Shut up!' grunted Slater, and the range boss slowly reseated himself but kept his hairy hands spread wide and flat upon the table top, in front of him. 'I been kind of wanting to have me another little talk with this boy,' Slater went on, in his heavy voice. 'Been hearing a lot about him, since that day we met here in this saloon. He's been cutting quite a swath.'

'You've heard some things, I dare say,' agreed Bill, shortly.

Slater gave his range boss a sideward look, that held cruel humour in it. 'I heard,' he said, 'that you braced a bunch of riders out on the Loops, that was making trouble for a Trent freight wagon. Heard you bad wounded one and chased the others off, singlehanded. Pretty good going!'

Noonan's thick chest swelled on a sharpdrawn breath; his broad features coloured. Looking at him, Bill allowed a corner of his mouth to flutter in a half-smile that did not quite shape itself.

'Not as impressive as it maybe sounds,' he protested, genially. 'They were a yellow-bellied lot. They were ready to scatter anyhow — scared off by a girl with a rifle . . .'

A strangled sound broke from Noonan, and someone at the bar who had probably been there on the Loops that day let go with a muffled oath. But Steve Slater had begun to laugh, swelling chuckles that shook his shoulders and upper body loosely. He was laughing at Noonan; the latter knew it and his thick fingers began to twitch with fury.

Then the laughter stopped and Slater had turned to Bill Dawson again. He said, bluntly, 'You're a pretty sharp boy, all right. Maybe I made a mistake turning you down for a job, that day. But maybe it ain't too late. How would you like to go to work for me?'

Dawson stared, suddenly realizing the man was in earnest. It was Slater's admission that he had proved too dangerous an adversary — and it was the highest flattery he had ever been paid. But though a refusal meant danger, Bill Dawson had no thought of hesitating.

'I got a job,' he said flatly. 'One I like real well.'

'With the Trents,' muttered Slater. His face had darkened, his voice gone quickly flinty. 'That's too bad, because you might not have that job long. I got a feeling the Trents ain't gonna be in business much after the first of the month.'

'Might be. Might not be, too. Reckon I'll stick it out,' Eyes hooded behind their lids, Steve Slater picked up his glass; set it down again. He said, 'I just don't like to see a smart young feller throw away his chances. I could pay you pretty good wages.'

'No thanks.'

Then Virg Noonan said, with coarse meaning: 'Aw, hell, Steve! You got nothin' but money to offer him — not the sort of wages he's likely gettin' from that yellow-haired wench down in Fair Play.'

Bill Dawson was on his feet — his face gone white, his whole body trembling. 'You filthy — !'

'Why, damn you!'

The chair toppled behind Virg Noonan, crashing, as he too came surging up, his right hand moving towards holster. He had been stung too far and the intent to kill was plain in his wild stare. And the speed of his draw was plain murder, when pitted against that of any ordinary man — a man, for example, like Bill Dawson who was no expert at all with the Bisley .45 at his own side.

But Dawson had no intention of matching a killer's draw. Instead, his eye had found the braided riding crop lying convenient, as always, to Noonan's hand, on the sticky table top. And as Noonan began his play, Dawson had shot out a hand and snatched the quirt, brought it up and sharply down. The weighted end landed, hard, on Noonan's gun-wrist just as his heavy Colt cleared leather; there was the audible thud of its striking and the gleaming smear of metal as the gun flew from numbed fingers, end over end, to pin-wheel with a smash against the bar and send the men there scattering out of the way of it.

Next instant, Bill Dawson was wading in and planting a fist square into the middle of Noonan's mouth. He felt the meaty lips crush beneath his knuckles, the sharp pain as they struck a tooth. And he heard the angry shouts that built from a half dozen throats, and descended upon him in an engulfing wave of peril.

12

He caught himself after the follow-through, the pain of that blow a tingling numbness that ran clear up into the elbow. Looking about quickly, he found every eye pinned upon him, every man in the room held in a jerky, taut-muscled stance and more than one hand drawn half-way towards a gun barrel. Yet no gun left leather, no man moved; and then he discovered why.

On his knees in the centre of the saw-dust-littered floor, Virg Noonan had one arm lifted to wave back the other Big S men. The other hand was pressed hard against his mouth, from which issued furious, animal-like grunts of pain and anger. And, between the thick fingers, a thread of bright crimson came seeping slowly.

He took the hand away, looked stupidly a moment at his own blood. Then, fumbling in front of him, he picked up a tiny object. He held it in his palm, and raised his head slowly to glare at Dawson. He said, thickly, 'I'll fix you for that! I'll bust you apart with my bare hands.'

Only then did Bill Dawson realize what the object was — when he saw the bloody gap it had left in the centre of the man's upper jaw.

'I told you once,' he grunted, 'to watch out if I ever got a fair chance at you! Now you can use that gold tooth for a collar stud, like I mentioned . . . '

With a curse, Virg Noonan flung the tooth from him. He ran a hairy wrist across the ruin of his mouth; next instant, he was driving up to his feet and making for Bill Dawson with big fists swinging.

Bill Dawson faded back, avoiding the sheer physical weight of that rush. None of the other Big S crew made any move towards him. It looked as though they were staying out, letting Noonan have this his way; apparently they expected to see no surprises. Neither, for that matter, did Bill.

Noonan on his feet was a grim sight for an opponent — even more impressive than Noonan in the saddle. He looked to the smaller man to have something the proportions of a tree, and Bill felt no shame as he used some quick foot-work to draw away from that advancing peril, despite the hoots the Big S men poured upon him with derisive orders to stand and fight.

But Noonan was fast, for all his size, and Bill didn't quite evade the reach of one of those massive fists. It took him on the cheek, tearing the skin as the knuckles slid away, and he felt as though half his face had gone with it.

Jarred, his responses were blurred and he stood there and let a chance for a return blow slip by while Noonan was still uncovered by the weight of his own wild swing. He had recovered before a second one came, however, and managed to duck away from it and into the clear, his head still ringing.

'Stand still, damn you!'

Virg Noonan was coming right after him, his thirst for punishing only whetted. Seeing an opening, Bill threw in a stabbing right that stung his opponent below the eye but bounced off the solid cheekbone. Then, still retreating, he felt the edge of the bar strike his back and quickly moved sideward to avoid being trapped against it.

He didn't quite make it. A toe hooked the brass railing at the base of the bar and tripped him so that he spun about in a wild circle, grabbing at the edge of the counter to right himself. While he was hanging like that, off balance, a sledging wallop from Noonan descended across the small of his back. It all but crippled him, slamming a good part of the wind out of his lungs. He went down rolling, and brought up against the underpinning of a table.

Lying there, gasping for lost breath while the room seemed to spin, he saw his enemy coming at him — saw a heavy cowhide boot lifting to drive into his prone body. He was blocked by the table from moving farther to escape it; reaching blindly, then, his fingers contacted an overturned chair and desperately he hurled this into Noonan's path. The big man collided with it and went down; the chair smashed to matchsticks under his beefy weight.

It gave Bill a moment and he fought to his feet, still sobbing wind into his lungs. Noonan was already disentangling himself from the wreckage of the chair and lurching upright.

Looking at the bloody face and the frightening size of him, Bill Dawson knew a frantic impulse to end the uneven struggle by grabbing for the gun that still, miraculously, rode the holster at his waist. But such a move, he knew, would bring the rest of the pack down on him, that were holding off only because of their confidence that the range boss could take care of him with those mauling, punishing fists.

So he left the gun alone and, overcoming his fierce reluctance to go back into that desperate fight, drove himself forward before Noonan could quite get ready for him.

The range boss had come up with a leg

of the splintered chair in one hand, like a club. Bill shouldered it aside and drove both fists, one after another, against the big man's unprotected jaw. It felt like sledging into a stone wall, but it held Noonan for a moment; and Bill Dawson lowered his attack and let him have it in the stomach. He rammed solid muscle; then, with the second blow, his fist sank in — wrist-deep, it felt like.

A groan broke from Noonan's battered mouth. The chairleg descended; Bill caught that on his forearm, which went instantly numb with pain. He slammed another fist into Noonan's ruined face and then he got a grip on the club and tore it out of his opponent's grasp and, without any compunction whatsoever, swung the splintered chairleg against Noonan's skull and watched him drop, knocked senseless.

He lifted his head quickly, to meet the angry looks of the Bar S men. 'He tried it first!' Bill Dawson pointed out hoarsely. 'Noonan was the first to grab a club. That made it fair for anybody!'

He dropped the chairleg beside Virg Noonan's crumpled form, and straightened slowly, running a sleeve across his bloody face.

A thundering quiet had descended on the room. The besting of Noonan was the last ending any of these Big S men had expected to that encounter, and the shock of it seemed to hold them and stay their hands and their very tongues. But it wasn't a respite that would last for long.

And so Bill Dawson seized the opportunity to slide his gun from holster, and drop its muzzle on big Steve Slater who had reached his feet now. Slater's thick features were expressionless; when he saw the gunbarrel swing towards him and heard it click sharply to full cock, his eyes flickered once but he made no move.

'Tell your men to hold off!' Bill Dawson snapped. 'Don't let anybody else mix into it, or I promise you'll be the first one hurt!'

Slater's mouth twisted. 'You're not getting off so damned easy! There's a half dozen against you, boy!'

'And I'm the one with a gun drawn and cocked — which I reckon gives me the edge all around! 'Bill flicked a look at the Big S crew. 'Maybe you'd better all shed those gunbelts! You first, Slater. Unbuckle yours and kick it under the table!'

It was touch and go, for a moment, whether the order would be heeded. Bill Dawson could feel his palm go slick with sweat, clamped tight around the Eisley. The punchers along the bar looked at Slater, and the latter glared at Bill defiantly. Then, however, the rancher's mouth twisted and he shrugged.

'Aw, hell! Let him go — he can't get far!' Big hands fumbled with a buckle, and the worn cartridge belt slid down Slater's thick legs, weighted holster thudding against the floor.

'Kick it!' murmured Bill Dawson.

With an angry growl, Slater obeyed. As the gun disappeared beneath the table, where it would take precious seconds to reach, Dawson looked meaningfully at the others. Without a word, they followed their boss's example; one by one, their guns went across the mahogany to strike the floor behind it. Bill glanced at the bartender, who quickly moved around to the front of the bar, his hands carefully at shoulder height.

Satisfied, Dawson sidled backward. His heel stepped on something and he saw it was his own hat, lost in that battle with Virg Noonan. He leaned and scooped it up, dragged it on.

Then he had reached the door, and with a quick move he wrenched it open, and ducked through.

He was already a dozen yards away before the loose pane of the slammed door stopped rattling. Then yells, the stampeding of booted feet, the crash of a table overturning warned him that his enemies were wasting no time in getting back their weapons. The racket doubled in volume, suddenly, as someone kicked the door open again, letting shouts spill out upon the quiet street.

Dawson wheeled, put his shoulders

flat against a building's clapboard front while he swung up his gunarm and punched two quick shots towards the saloon. A man had appeared in the doorway but the near whine of the bullets sent him jerking back inside again. And Bill Dawson went on.

This was cutting it mighty thin. His wagon and teams, fortunately, were ready to go — and also, fortunately, pointed in the right direction down the steep and rutted hill. It was a matter simply of getting to the driver's seat, booting off the brake, yelling the horses to a start. But there were some thirty yards to cover, and even if he did make the wagon the Big S men had horses waiting, handy, at the hitching rail before the saloon. The mood they were in, he knew they would quickly overtake him, and shoot him off the box.

Even now, a gun, behind him, laid its racket against the sounding boards of false building fronts. The bullet did not come even close, but a quick, cold sweat broke out upon Bill Dawson's body and his back muscles knotted in a spasm of dread. His heel slipped in slick mud and he went down, sprawling, catching himself with his hands; he scrambled up again, fighting against panic. The big wagon seemed suddenly beyond reach . . .

Then, up from the foot of the long street, a trio of riders came boiling. They were upon Bill Dawson almost before he saw them or was even aware of the hoof-sound; they burst into view pulling wide around the endgate of the freight wagon; and one yelled at him in the voice of Dave Burke: 'Dawson! Hey, man! Get going!'

'We'll hold them off!' It was Frank Harris, adding his shout to Burke's. 'Try to get that rig to rolling, will you?'

Astonishment jarred through him that these men of South Renner should suddenly have appeared from nowhere to bring him desperately needed aid. They had jerked reins now and were trying to hold their horses quiet while they worked their guns, and the Big S men, pinned within the saloon by their fire, were shooting back.

A window smashed; the horses tied to the hitch pole added their shrill terror to the confusion of guns. Elsewhere along the street, Bill Dawson glimpsed startled faces peering from doors and windows but no sign of any man daring enough to venture out into this suddenly bursting gunfight.

Dawson, meanwhile, was taking full advantage of the break that had been offered him: if these farmers were risking their necks to give him a chance, he knew he had to make the best use of it and waste no second of precious time. Now he had reached the freight outfit, and hurriedly unsnapped the iron weight that held the lead team anchored. The horses were frightened, uneasy at the guns. Bill hauled his sore body up to the seat, took the jerkline in one painfully swollen fist as his boot found the brake and kicked it hard. 'Take off, doggone you!' he shouted, in a voice hoarse with excitement.

For an instant he thought they were

going to tangle in the harness, but after that he had them straightened out and his hollering, added to the gun-roar, got them running. With a down-hill start, the frightened teams went tearing away from there at a rattling pace, the empty wagon rumbling and jouncing and once nearly capsizing as its off wheels hit bottom in a deep rut.

Bill Dawson seldom used a whip but he was using one now, its poppers scorching the air above his teams' laid-back ears. Then, nearing the end of the street where it levelled and became the north-south valley road, he looked back and saw that his benefactors were spurring hard in the wake of the big wagon. Uphill, Slater's men were spilling out of the saloon, making a knot of activity at the hitch rail as they tried to calm their horses enough to get into saddle.

Dave Burke came kicking his horse up even with the rig and leaned to shout above the uproar: 'Keep 'em running! We got a little start and if we can get this outfit to the boundary fence, we can hold Slater off there.'

'They'll soon overtake the wagon,' Bill yelled back. 'Should they manage to plug one of the teams, that will pile her up for fair. Thanks for helping me out of a fight — but now you better start covering distance.'

'We'll stick around, see if we can't hold 'em back. If we aren't able to save the wagon, then I'll take you up behind me. This nag will carry double.'

Before Dawson could answer he had dropped behind again, to join the others. Bill's hands were full managing the teams and the clumsy, jouncing wagon, but his ears tingled with the expectation and waiting for the renewal of gunfire.

The horses were running strongly, in a steady rhythm of bobbing heads and flanks. The road boiled past, the forground of new-green rangeland blurred with the speed of passage, wheeling ever more slowly as it receded towards the vanishing point where timbered hills and far peaks stood motionless. There was little dust but the shod hoofs kicked up grit and mud, spattering him, keeping his eyes slit-shut until his cheek muscles pinched and fluttered with the painful effort. Once, peering back along the dark tunnel of the wagon-body and through the tawny film that sifted behind the rear bow, he had a glimpse of the dark mass of Big S riders, far to the rear but steadily drawing nearer.

Then the first shots sounded.

The distance was still too great for targeting from the back of a speeding horse, so the wagon's escort did not waste lead by attempting a reply. But there was no question now of Steve Slater's intentions. He meant to have the hide of this upstart drifter who had defied him and beaten up his tough foreman — and it would be too bad for anyone who interfered.

Suddenly, Bill remembered the rifle Lila Trent had insisted he carry in the wagon with him, in a scabbard strapped to the dashboard at his feet. Laying aside the whip he slid the weapon out. Accurate shooting from this pitching, swaying vehicle was a poor proposition but it seemed worth a try, especially as none of the pursuing cattlemen appeared to have a saddle gun. Dawson left the horses to their own devices while he twisted about and, kneeling on the seat, put the stock to his shoulder and tried to draw a bead. The target bobbed crazily; he fought the pitch and jounce of the wagon. Half blindly, he worked the trigger.

The lash of the weapon was slapped back at him by the prisoning wagon canvas; but he saw a sudden gap in that knot of horsemen and knew he must have scored a lucky hit. Encouraged and half unbelieving, he quickly flipped the ejector, fired again and again. Two shots were wasted, in quick succession, but then a couple of horses went crashing together, as a rider failed to pull free in time to miss tangling with the bullet-struck mount just ahead.

After that the Big S riders were hastily fanning out, offering less of a target; however they had also taken caution and were slowing a little to draw out of range. As a consequence the wagon teams seemed almost to plunge ahead, widening the distance.

With a tight grin of triumph, Dawson laid aside his rifle and turned again to work on the horses.

13

Now Dave Burke came pulling even with him, shouting across the racket of the wheels: 'They've dropped out of sight! That rifle did it. They've fallen back to look after the men you dropped.'

Looking back, Dawson discovered that this was actually so. The road behind was empty of riders, and they showed nowhere on the rolling flats of bunchgrass. He used his jerkline, therefore, and brought the horses gradually to a slower pace and then halted them to stand blowing, sweat runnelling down their twitching legs and into the mud of the road.

'I've got to rest them,' he told Burke. 'I can't run them all the way to the fence without a break! They'll die in the traces!'

The other pair of riders had joined Burke around the wagon. Frank Harris, fighting his restless horse, cried, 'I doubt if we got much time. Slater's out for blood; he'll be after us again in a minute.'

'Then I'll use that minute! I've got to take this team through. If you want to keep going, it's all right. Maybe I can make it in by myself.'

'Nothing doing,' young Burke said, doggedly. 'It was Jean sent us after you, and she told me she'd never speak to me again if you were to get in trouble with Big S and we didn't help you out of it — after all you'd done for us. Jean figures we owe you a debt.'

Dawson said, 'Well, if you ever did it's squared now!'

He looked around at the three. Frank Harris had a bullet nicked ear that was bleeding pretty freely, but he seemed to be paying no mind to it. Burke and the other one, a youngster named Ty Rogers, didn't seem to have been hurt. So far, they had come through very well and for this he was humbly grateful.

He jumped down and went along the line of horses, checking on the condition of his teams to discover how they were bearing up. They had had a good graining in Renner City and he figured they had enough bottom left to get as far as the wire. He hoped so anyway . . .

Rogers suddenly lifted a cry: 'They're coming! And they've picked up reinforcements!'

At a run, Dawson headed back to the wagon and scrambled up. Shouting and slapping their hats against the rumps of the teams, the other pair already had them started. Bill expertly got them straightened out in a mile-consuming run.

Guns were popping behind them, but too far away. Big S had indeed picked up more men somewhere but respect for the rifle was holding them back; they didn't know that the weapon contained only a few more shots, and that Dawson had no extra ammunition for it.

The walls of rock and timber were narrowing now, pinching together in a way that told him the barbed wire barricade lay not far ahead — the four slim strands that spelled safety. Bill Dawson took heart from this, certain now that his teams would last it out despite the futile chase by the Big S men, and the fanatic fury of Slater that egged them on.

Suddenly Frank Harris was voicing a yell of warning: 'Ahead of us! Watch it!'

Almost at the same moment, Dawson saw them — other riders, shifting through a thin screen of timber that tongued out from the encroaching valley wall; and he understood. The road swerved close to these trees, and during the halt Slater had sent part of his men circling to wait there while the others herded the wagon and its escort into their guns. On the ground, and behind cover, they would have little trouble picking the riders from saddle, or at least dropping one of the freight team and crippling the wagon.

'Pull out!' cried Dawson, swinging an arm in a wide movement. And he grabbed the check-line.

For a few strides the canny near leader resisted the pull of the line. Then, as Dawson repeated his signal insistently, it gave in and swung to the left. Another moment and they were off the road, heading straight across country.

Sage clumps and brush whipped against the turning wheels; uneven ground and buried rocks sent the empty rig jouncing and threatening a spill or a smash-up, which at this speed could mean death for horses and driver alike. But somehow the wagon stayed upright and that threatening tongue of woods was being passed up by a wide margin, beyond gun-reach.

But, seeing the failure of their ambush, the Big S gunmen were quickly hurling themselves into leather now; and here they came, out of the trees — four of them, cutting straight towards the wagon and bearing in quickly.

There was no chance to use the rifle; he had his hands too full and the crazy careening of the rig made using it out of the question. But Dave Burke was leaning from saddle, an arm extended. 'Quick! Pass it over!'

Dawson grabbed the gun and shoved it

into the other's hand. Guns were already yammering as the quartet from the trees closed in. Suddenly the rifle in Burke's hands added its voice. He had aimed for the mounts, a rider being too difficult to target; and he sent one crashing into the sage. The rest of the men, not being fools, scattered apart. The wagon swept on, unmolested.

Moments later the brown road-ribbon came swooping towards them and the wagon — still upright, by some miracle — dropped into it, and the teams leaped forward over the better going. And just ahead, Bill Dawson caught the gleam of four-strand wire and knew they had won. For with only a narrow gate through the barrier commanded by the pile-up of talus rock anchoring either end, it would not take many guns to lay a field of fire across that bottle-neck — enough to halt an army.

And the Big S riders, falsely confident that those men in the trees could do the trick, had dropped too far behind to hope to stop the fugitives now. They spurted forward but it was too late.

Nevertheless, Bill Dawson never knew a more welcome sensation than in the moment when he went skidding through the opening in the wire, and a yell of triumph told him that his escort, too, had reached its safety. He took a curve on two wheels, putting his rig and teams into the shelter of talus boulders that tumbled down into the narrow gap, and brought the winded horses to a stand.

Frank Harris and Rogers were leaning from their saddles to haul the double panels of the gate to and fasten them. Dave Burke halted alongside the wagon, his face a little pale under its coating of dust and sweat, but his eyes sparkling.

'We made it!' he grunted. He held his reins and the smoking rifle in one hand, favouring his left arm which was still a little stiff. The sorrel between his knees was blowing hard and nearly exhausted; it had been a cruel, tough job for the horses.

'They may be on us in a minute, though.'

The farmer jerked his head towards the rocks. 'We can hole up there and stop any try they might want to make against the fence. They'll never get past.'

'That's my figuring.'

Harris rode up, and Burke told him, 'Why don't you ride to send some help to us here? And then have that ear tended to.'

'What ear?' Looking puzzled, Harris touched both members, wincing in pain and surprise and then staring blankly at the blood that came away on his hand. 'Well what do you know! I never felt that tag me!'

'It didn't miss far tagging you for good,' said Dawson, bleakly. 'Slater means business. I'm afraid this could be the big one — the open start of war between you and B S . . . and all because you sided me today!'

Frank Harris grunted sourly. 'What's happened today has small bearing on it. Slater's been intending a war with us, sooner or later. If it comes now, it'll be because he wants it now.' He picked up

the reins. 'I'll get the word around, fast.'
He rode off, a blood-soaked handker-
chief clamped against his hurt ear.

Over at the fence, Ty Rogers lifted a
sudden cry. 'They're comin'!'

Sure enough, out there beyond the
barrier a skirmish line had formed and
was moving up, without haste. Sunlight
struck bright glints from gunbarrels carried openly, and from saddle trappings
and one man's big, Mexican spur rowel.

'Into the rocks!' ordered Burke. 'Ty,
you take the other side; the two of us will
fort up here.'

Bill Dawson was already scrambling
down from the wagon seat. Burke, dis-
mounting, tossed him the rifle and he
caught it by the balance, went climbing
hurriedly to a place of vantage in the
tumbled boulders.

Thirty feet above the level of the gap,
he found a likely spot behind a flat-
topped ledge and slid into it; an instant
later Dave Burke joined him. Bill laid
his rifle across the flat rock and placed
his six-gun beside it. Across the gap, Ty

Rogers waved an arm to signal that he was in place and ready, and Dave Burke lifted his own hand in answer.

They waited, then, watching the horsemen draw slowly nearer.

Until that moment, in the excitement of chase and battle, Bill Dawson had hardly been aware of his body. Now the soreness and ache of battered flesh began to creep insidiously into his consciousness. He flexed the fingers of his right hand, grimacing; he thought he could almost hear the bones scraping against one another and hoped he hadn't cracked a knuckle in that vicious fight with Noonan.

His cheek was tender and raw, his right forearm badly bruised where the blow of a clubbed chairleg had struck; while every move of shoulder muscles and every deep breath he drew put an ache through his upper body as a result of a single, pummelling smash of Noonan's fist against the middle of his back . . .

Suddenly Dave Burke, beside him, was sending his shout across the stillness:

'I think that's far enough, Slater!'

Some fifty yards from the fence, the line of horsemen kept coming despite the warning; but a moment later the Big S boss seemed to think better of the thing, and with an upflung hand, brought his men to a halt. There were a half dozen of them now, with Slater's bulky frame at their centre,

He hurled his hoarse voice at the men all but invisible in the rocks. 'You telling me where I can or can't ride?'

'We're just telling you where we think you'd be safer!'

At that, Steve Slater showed signs of losing his temper. 'Why, you damned, upstart nesters! You been asking for trouble, and I've held my hand. But don't try to defy me now! That Dawson half killed Virg Noonan, and I mean him to pay; so, send him out here!'

Bill started to frame an answer, but Dave Burke beat him out with a stern rejection. 'Nothing doing! If he wants to go, that's up to him. It's all right, too, if you figure you want to try coming in after him — only, I wouldn't advise it.'

'Oh, you wouldn't?' The Big S boss lifted in the stirrups, and raising a fist he shook it angrily. 'All right, then! You've had your warning, and you've gone too far. Now, I'm giving you a final ultimatum — and twelve hours to think it over! By tomorrow morning I want this wire down; if it's not, and I have to tear it down by force, I promise I'll also stamp out every stinking homestead in South Renner!'

Ty Rogers shouted from the other side of the gap, 'That'll take some tall stampin', mister!' But Dave Burke did not bother to put his answer into words. Instead he grabbed up the rifle from under Dawson's hand, flipped a cartridge into the breach and, with stock to cheek, triggered off a shell that furrowed the air not more than a few inches from Slater's head.

The Big S boss ducked wildly; with a last shake of his fist, Slater reined about and stabbed his grey saddler with the spurs.

None of his men had any desire to brace a rifle. The lot of them were at his heels as he rode back up the valley, quickly merging with the long shadow of the western rim; the sound of their horses soon lost itself in the murmur of the pines, where the first chill winds of evening were already stirring.

Letting out a long breath, Dave Burke jacked out the spent cartridge and handed the rifle back to Dawson. His expression was serious but showed no fear. 'That's that,' he muttered. 'It was bound to happen, sooner or later.'

'The wire won't be coming down, then?'

'What do *you* think? That's too steep a price to pay for peace — if peace is what you'd call the thing we've got here! Those four strands of barbed wire, alone, have kept our land for us. Get our wheat into the ground once, and starting up and then see the quick work Slater's herds could make of it. One well-planned stampede, across our fields, is all it would take.'

Soberly, Bill Dawson had to admit that he had called it right. There could be no turning back . . .

14

All through that night, as a precaution against possible surprise, a fire was kept burning in a shelter point in the rocks and a two-man relief stood guard over the fence. And, lasting until a late hour, the men of South Renner held a emergency session in their usual meeting place — Tom McHail's kitchen.

When they all gathered there they filled it near to overflowing; and there was a certain similarity in every sun-darkened face, in its grave seriousness and foreboding what lay ahead. Hardly one of them had any dissenting comment on the general decision, which was fully and soberly confirmed in open discussion. This, each man agreed, was the showdown; and better to have it so.

Better to learn now, rather than at some future date, if they were to be allowed to complete the building of their dream here in Renner . . . or if Slater's ruthless greed was to crush them and drive them out.

Bill Dawson, listening intently to every word of the discussion, raised a point of strategy. 'If you're able to hold Slater back from the fence — and I think he would be a fool to suppose you can't — what other chances has he? Is there any way he can sneak his men in here without your being prepared for it?'

'I can't see how,' McHail answered him. 'We're well situated for defence. The rims are too high and too steep to come across the wall, except in one or two places; and we'll keep an eye on those. We got plenty of ammunition. If we block both entrances to the valley we'll be out of his reach unless, of course, he has some scheme up his sleeve that we aren't able to guess at.'

'That's a possibility you better hadn't miss,' agreed Dawson. He added, seriously, 'You don't know how badly I feel about what's happened today. Maybe so the trouble was bound to come — but the fact remains it did come because I

266

went up to Renner City and got myself caught in a jam, and needed your help to pull me loose from it. And now I can't even stay tomorrow morning to face the thing out with you with too much work waiting to be done, down below.

'Still, I think you realize we're all in this fight, and we'll stick it out — you folks, and me, and the Trents. It's like Jabez pointed out: we're small, and we're fighting somebody that's pretty big. But together, maybe we can keep whittling at Steve Slater until we bring him down to a size where we can knock him over. It's a cinch, if we don't stand up to him, then this section ain't going to be a place worth living in and we aren't going to have much excuse to call ourselves men.'

'I'll say 'amen' to that!' someone agreed, fervently. And on that note the decision was taken, the meeting adjourned.

With morning, an increasing tension lay on every nester home in South Renner. More than one man had lain sleepless through the long hours, not moving, feigning sleep because he had not wanted to reveal his uneasiness to the woman who lay beside him — herself, likely as not, equally wide-eyed and listening for the breathing of her children, and wondering what the new dawn would bring to them. When the flush of sunrise colours swelled the steel-grey sky, they looked at one another and rose to the day's normal chores; trying not to show by their manner the tightness that was in them; but their unnatural silences showed it anyway.

Up to the time Bill Dawson took his departure for the railhead at Fair Play, however, nothing had happened to justify this anxiety. The guard on the fence had been strengthened and was on the alert for a first sign of trouble, but the deadline Slater had set came and passed without event, or any word of activity on the Big S side of the line. Bill delayed his leaving as long as he could; then, with morning half gone, he had to succumb to the pressures of his job and reluctantly pull out, promising the McHail's that he would be waiting for any word that they needed him.

And still time dragged out for the people of South Renner.

An air of brooding settled like a fog over the timbered trough of the valley — a fog which the warmth of the rising sun could not touch or dissipate. The day had turned out clear and fine, invigorating for a man with good, hard work before him; only, no man could give his attention fully to this work, from wondering what Slater meant to do.

The sun mounted, morning waxed and ebbed. Once a Big S rider came within sight of the fence and sat saddle for a space of minutes, a distant figure that brought the guards to quick alertness; but he came no nearer than that, and after a bit turned his horse and rode away again. They decided he must have been sent to check and determine if any action had been taken to conform with Slater's ultimatum. The strands of the fence, shining still under the high sunlight, would give him answer enough.

They had nearly decided Slater meant

to let them wait like this, sweating out his decision, perhaps for days and taking his own time to make any move; but then, towards noon, the watchers spotted horsemen approaching. There were ouly two of them. One was Slater, himself; the second they identified, after a moment's puzzled wait, when they saw the stab of sunlight reflected from metal, in the gap of his unbuttoned coat.

'Ward Kyle!' grunted old McHail, who was among the men at the fence line. 'So Slater brought his sheriff with him, from Renner City, instead of guns. He's got something cute up his sleeve — that much is plain!'

One of the others fingered a long-barrelled Colt, nervously. 'What do we do?' he muttered.

'Let them come as far as the fence. Looks like they want to parley. I'll have to see what's on their minds . . . '

When he reached the point where Bill Dawson's rifle had halted him the afternoon before, Steve Slater put up a hand and called across the stillness: 'We're ridin' in, and our guns are in our holsters. If you shoot now it's murder!'

'Ride ahead!' Tom McHail yelled. To his own men he said, 'Cover me,' and with Dave Burke at his side walked out from the rocks to meet Steve Slater and the lawman, only the barbed barricade of the fence to separate them.

Boots set wide apart, the old man glared up at the horsemen. He said coldly, 'Well, we didn't take down any wire.'

'I got eyes,' snapped Slater, with a manner of one who tries without complete success to hold on to his temper. 'I can see what you did and didn't do. I had an idea it would be like this.'

'That's good! I'm glad we understand each other!'

'I ain't so sure we do. I said I wanted this wire out of here. I meant I intended it should come out.'

Dave Burke suggested, 'If you got a pair of nail-pullers on you, just go right ahead and try your hand. Why don't you?'

'Because I'd rather watch you do it.' He turned to the sheriff. 'Show 'em that paper, Ward.'

Ward Kyle was already taking it from his pocket, unfolding it with nervous fingers. Kyle was not a young man, or one with much strength of will; if he had been, it is doubtful that he would have served so many years in an office where his official hands were tied to the dominance and wishes of a bully like Slater.

'This here is a court order,' he said, clearing his throat first. 'Issued by Judge Hawkins in Renner City, in behalf of the people of this county. It says the fence is to come down immediately.'

'Yes?' Old Tom McHail's sharp eye was squinted; one hard hand came up and began to pull at the flowing white whiskers — a sure sign that anger was boiling in him. 'What have 'the people' got to do with this?'

'Why, you're obstructing a major artery of commerce. No one has the right to impede the flow of traffic on a public road. It's all written down here.'

Sheriff Kyle offered him the paper. 'And I'm supposed to see that you do like it says.'

'So that's it!' Dave Burke took the legal paper from his father-in-law, looked at it with a bleak tightness in the muscles of his jaw. 'I guess they've got us.'

The smug look of triumph that slid across Steve Slater's wide face, at this admission, faded somewhat when Tom McHail retorted sharply, 'Nothing of the sort! This fence has a gate, and the gate hasn't got any lock. It's no obstruction to traffic and was never intended as such. Judge Hawkins knows why it was put up; to save our fields from drift cattle. We've got a legal right to do that — you can look it up in the books.'

Sheriff Kyle seemed to be wavering a little, but Slater's stare hardened. 'This road is my drive trail to market. You can't fence my beef off of it.'

'You drive no beef this time of year, and you know it. By fall we'll have wire on all our crops and then the fence can come down. Not until then! And no piece of paper,' McHail added, stabbing a finger at the injunction, 'is going to make any difference. We'll fight it in any court you want to take it to!'

The Big S boss looked at Ward Kyle. 'Looks like it's your move, Sheriff.'

'Well, now . . . ' The lawman stirred in the saddle, an unhappy look on him. 'Singlehanded, I don't rightly know how I can enforce an order like this — not if they're bound on resisting it. They got all the advantage.'

'Send for help!'

'An army couldn't bust through this fence!' Dave Burke retorted sharply. 'I'd think you and your tough crew found that out for yourselves, last evening.'

Slater said, 'Suppose I was to ask the governor to order in the state militia?'

'We'd like it fine!' snapped McHail, catching him up. 'We'd like nothing better than to have someone here with authority to make you keep your stock on your own side of the line, where it belongs, so that we could all get back to our planting! No, Slater! That's *one* threat we know you haven't any intention of carrying out. You don't want anyone from outside getting wind of what you're trying to do up here! As for the road, it's wide open to everybody but Big S; and it's even open to you — except that any Big S rider is going to have to take his gun off, before he can ride through the gate.'

Colour had mounted angrily into Slater's broad features. 'Take off our guns?' he repeated, thunderously. 'To be massacred, I suppose, by you stubble jumpers?'

'You know better than that. So does the sheriff, I reckon. We're peaceable folk, given neighbours who'll leave us alone. There's nothing treacherous in our way of fighting — but we'll fight hard, if crowded!'

Ward Kyle turned a helpless look on the Big S boss. 'If they just won't listen to a court order,' he said, 'there's nothing more I can do, either alone or with a posse. I don't want to see men needlessly killed, as they would be trying to open this road by force. But the governor, now — '

'No!' Steve Slater appeared, all at once, to have shaped a decision. With a quick movement he slipped his six-gun out of holster and extended it, butt first, to the sheriff. 'I'm being a fool, but I'll give them a chance. I'll risk my neck to see if they mean what they say. Take the gun! I'm riding through the gate — alone! I'm heading clear across South Renner. I dare 'em to stop me!'

The lawman looked at the gun, then accepted it with reluctance. Tom McHail nodded his bearded head. 'Dave, open up the gate!' he ordered. 'Our word is good, Slater! Act in good faith and there'll be no trouble with us . . . but try trickery of any kind, and you'll learn our answer to that quick enough!'

'Maybe I better come with you, Steve,' the sheriff suggested, uneasily.

Slater shook his head. 'Ride on back. I'm heading down to Fair Play; got business there. If I don't return in a couple of days, you can figure maybe I never made it!'

He ticked steel to his grey, and rode deliberately forward towards the gate which Dave Burke had opened at the old man's order. The farmers drew aside as he came through. Slater looked at neither man, nor at the tumbled rocks where he knew that other guns, in nervous fingers, covered his movements.

Erect in the saddle, eyes straight ahead, he rode into South Renner, straight down the wagon road. And if there was fear in him, nothing of it showed.

★ ★ ★

In Fair Play, which he hit sometime after darkness had settled over the flat sage-lands, Steve Slater knew his way around well enough. He knew, also, where he could find the type of men he needed for the scheme that had taken shape in his fertile brain, during the long ride down from the hills. Near the railroad tracks there was a solid block of cheap saloons, frequented by the floating population of tramps and thugs and hard cases that rode the rods and the boxcars. Here, the proper amount of cash could easily buy as many such as might be needed, for any kind of proposition.

A half hour of cautious talk with certain men that he singled out as likely prospects, and a few dollars peeled from the thick roll he generally carried, satisfied him that he had things building as he wanted them. There was one other man yet to be consulted, but Slater was so sure of this one that he figured the matter as good as settled; so he stopped for a good, solid meal in one of the town's eat shacks before going on to look up Tag Klebold, at the freight yard.

This place had changed considerably since Slater last set eyes on it. There was the smell of new lumber and new paint, and the light of a lantern swinging from a pole in the big yard showed him the rebuilt barn and the big, freshly-painted sign across the archway. Slater smiled secretly to himself, amused by all this. Through the office window he could see

Klebold's hunched figure seated at his desk. Slater went up the two plank steps, shoved the door open without knocking, and walked solidly inside; a blank, startled look on the freighter's gaunt face was his greeting.

'Well,' said the Big S boss, looking around with that same tight smile of amusement warping his mouth. 'Spreading out some, aren't you, Tag?'

Klebold laid the chewed stub of a pencil into the spine of an account book he had been struggling over, closed the book and pushed it aside into the other litter of the desk. Dark suspicion had replaced the first astonishment in his narrow face.

'What do you want here?'

His visitor gave him a close, speculative glance. 'You don't act very cordial. Not like the last time I seen you.'

'The last time I seen you,' retorted Klebold, 'you kicked me off your place.'

Slater dismissed this with a shrug. 'Things have changed since then. Sure looks as though they have for you; really rolling in money now, huh, Tag? Maybe, in that case, you aren't interested any more in getting my business . . . '

'I'm doing all right,' said the other, cautiously. 'Of course I'm always glad to pick up another good account.'

'Aw, hell! Let's cut out the big talk! You haven't grown that big, Klebold . . . you still need me and you know it. My backing will put you up where nobody can touch you — where Trent was, before he started crossing me. Trent's through, now, and you can take his place if you want . . . if you'll play ball. I'm here to tell you how.'

Klebold looked down at the raw-boned hands that were knotted, nervously, on top of the desk in front of him. 'I'm managing pretty good,' he repeated doggedly, 'on my own. Maybe I don't want to be tied to you. Maybe some day you'd do to me what you have to the Trents . . . '

With a quick stride Slater had reached the desk and was leaning forward with his big hands spread upon it, his face thrust into Klebold's.

'And how would you like to see a third

wagon outfit started here?' he demanded harshly. 'You wouldn't last a year if I decided to run you off the trails! You know that I reckon. The freighting business in this country is going to be run the way I say it is; I've got plans along that line, as soon as I've finished throwing those nesters out of my dooryard, up in Renner. Now, the question for you to make up your mind about — and damned quick — is whether it's going be you or somebody else that has a part in those plans!'

He straightened, his face granite-hard, and stabbed a finger at the door. 'If the answer is no — if you let me walk through there without agreeing to do the job I've arranged for you — then you'll never have a second chance to turn me down. So don't try to stall. This is it . . . this is final! Good night, Tag.'

Straightening, he turned abruptly towards the door. His hand was already on the knob before Tag Klebold surrendered with a groan of humiliation.

'All right — damn you! What's the

job, Slater?'

As he came back, Slater's hard mouth held smug amusement. 'You're easy to read,' he grunted, dragging a chair to the desk and slacking his heavy weight into it. 'I knew you didn't have the guts to let that door close behind me . . . I knew you weren't that big a fool!'

15

When the Big S boss had finished talking, Tag Klebold's bony face was left colourless and pasty-looking, and with a thin film of perspiration that shone greasily in the lampglow. He lifted an uncertain hand, ran it down across gaunt, sucked in cheeks. 'I — I dunno!' he muttered. 'This . . . I don't like anything about it!'

'Still, you'll do it,' replied Slater, with calm assurance. 'You'll do it because I tell you — and because I'm going to be right there to see you carry out your orders. Everything's arranged; the men we need are hired. I'll find a rider tonight to get word up to Virg Noonan and the boys at Big S so they'll be ready when the fence guard has been knocked out. You only follow instructions.'

'But . . . if something went wrong — if somebody guessed!'

Steve Slater brushed this aside with the cut of a heavy palm, as he shoved to his feet. 'Nothing will go wrong, and nobody will guess. Or if they do, it won't get them a damned thing. So quit worrying, and start thinking about doing your part of the job. I'll be back again in the morning.'

A moment later he had left, and the door closed firmly behind him.

Klebold let him go, throat dry and beyond speech. He sat the way he was for a long minute, merely staring at the panels; then with a convulsive lunge he reached for a drawer of the desk, and brought up a pint of whiskey, nearly full. He thumbed out the cork, put the mouth of the bottle to his lips and drank deeply of the raw stuff.

To his first shocked reaction, the plan Steve Slater had outlined seemed fantastic. There were so many ifs to it that a slipup, anywhere along the line, could spell disaster and ruin. He wondered for a dismal moment if Slater's reason had slipped, and an ego swollen with power had lost contact with reality; but then, calming, he told himself this couldn't be so. The Big S boss was the same crafty, brainy schemer that he had always been, and this latest plan merely reflected the man's consummate nerve and unflinching faith in himself.

Somewhat braced by this reflection and the liquor he had drunk, Tag Klebold corked the bottle and replaced it in its drawer while he went over the programme again, carefully, step by step. Yes, it was full of chances — and yet the sheer audacity of it made failure actually unlikely. Slater had thought of everything, he had weighed the odds and found the balance tipped in favour of success. And for a man like Slater, with so much dependent on an early and complete victory over the South Renner farmers, that was enough.

And, supposing the scheme worked, Tag Klebold would then know so much that Slater would never afterwards dare cut loose from him. Their futures would be inextricably linked, and whatever fortune Steve Slater reaped, Tag Klebold could demand his share — and get it.

So thinking, Klebold had shaken much of his initial panic as he rose and got his hat, blew the desk lamp and let himself out of the building.

Quiet lay upon the wagon yard, under the spray of yellow light from the lantern on its high post. The redhead, O'Shay, came from the barn and nodded greeting to his employer before passing out through the wide yard entrance. Someone was doing repair work on one of Klebold's big wagons; the stroke of the hammer, within the barn, brought him a sense of proprietorship that was very pleasing.

This prospering freight business that had so recently been a no-account, shoestring proposition, was his; and there would be even better to come. Smugly sure of himself now, his doubts of a few moments ago all but forgotten, Klebold strolled out of the yard and headed for the boarding house where he had his room and meals.

It was like a dash of cold water in the face when, a couple of blocks later, he suddenly caught sight of Bill Dawson emerging from a store opposite with a purchase of some description tucked beneath his arm.

Tag Klebold hauled up, staring across at that hated figure. He had lost all sight of Bill Dawson, during the scene with Slater and afterwards; he had almost forgotten that the man existed. Now, Klebold felt a twinge of fear.

In every encounter so far, that fiddle-foot had bested him. Even in the matter of the Trent wagons, where he had felt such high triumph over the advantage he had taken of his rivals' business troubles, on reflection he could not be sure that Dawson had not somehow secretly bested him; and the thought had soured his moment of triumph. Dawson was simply too sharp for him, and he had an uncanny way of seeming to know what was in a man's head despite the hardest effort at deceit.

All at once, the confidence Klebold had been enjoying in Steve Slater's brilliant scheming took a sharp sag. When you had a man like Bill Dawson against you, confidence was a treacherous luxury. You might get by with a daring proposition; but on the other hand there was a terrific risk. A risk that would be infinitely lessened if that drifter could be taken out of the picture . . .

Bill Dawson had halted almost directly opposite where Klebold stood; a match sprang to life as he fired up a cigarette. It showed his face clearly for a long moment, and then he shook it out and threw the stick away. And Klebold found that, half unconsciously, he had brought his six-gun out of holster and was gripping it so tightly that the muscles of his bony hand were beginning to cramp.

Then Dawson had moved on, and Klebold let the gun lower, forcing the tautness out of him. Still, an idea had been implanted in his crafty brain and his face was a taut, stiff mask as he stood there in the darkness, hearing the retreating sound of those other boots along the boardwalk. And suddenly Tag Klebold was starting forward, angling across the dark street at a cautious prowl in the wake of the other man.

He reached the farther walk, stepping up onto the planking as the man he was trailing turned a corner. The side street, too, was deserted and with only a small amount of light that spilled from doors and windows. Yet Tag Klebold stopped for a careful look around him before following Dawson into it.

Again Dawson had stopped, somewhere ahead; the muffled tread of his footsteps no longer sounded. With a high tension through his gaunt belly, Klebold faded forward, keeping close to the dark buildings. A cold bead of sweat ran trickling down across his ribs from below one armpit. Fear was high in him but the whiskey kept him going, building his resolve to finish this job that had been thrust into his hands.

He knew that a single shot, well placed, was all he would need to remove this most dangerous of enemies; he knew also that unless he took the opportunity now that it had presented itself, he would never work himself to this pitch of daring a second time . . .

Then his jaw clicked sharply on a sucked-in breath, for he had caught the indecipherable hum of voices in the quiet. Dawson must have encountered someone he knew. Klebold drew back against a wall, waiting in uncertainty, and already the resolution that had been so strong in him a moment before was slowly oozing out like air from a pricked balloon. He sensed this weakening, and despised himself for it.

Abruptly the talk had ceased, on grunted 'goodnights'. Dawson was continuing along the dark street, while the second man came on towards the place where Klebold waited. Satisfied that he was invisible in the piled shadows against the building front, the latter stayed there to let him pass. But, as luck would have it, in the instant before the man drew even with him someone within the building struck a light, and lampglow flooded through a window, directly upon them both.

The other's head jerked quickly; their eyes met. The man was Ed Strawhorn.

A moment later, and the marshal had gone on without saying a word; but once he stopped and turned for another curious look at Klebold. The freighter cursed inwardly. Upstreet, Bill Dawson was nearly out of hearing but he knew he could not go after him now — not after letting Ed Strawhorn see him loitering in the shadows. The lawman would remember if anything happened to Dawson tonight. He was a strong Trent supporter, and thus no friend of Tag Klebold's. And he would put two and two together.

So, with a savage anger at a chance wasted, Tag Klebold shoved his gun back into its holster and resumed his homeward course. But a gnawing conviction tormented him, telling him his having missed this chance at his enemy was going, somehow, to spell disaster . . .

★ ★ ★

291

Bill Dawson would have been much surprised to learn how narrowly he missed an ambush shot from the darkness that night. He was not one who had known cause to guard his back, or avoid shadowed and lonely sidestreets — no enemy had ever attached so much importance to the removal of a mere fiddle-foot. He might, in fact, have been oddly flattered had he known. But most likely, he would have been angry enough to go storming over to Klebold's and tear the place to pieces.

He did not know, however, and when he walked into the freight yard next day it was on an entirely different errand. He found Klebold standing in the spring sunshine, gaunt, thin-blooded frame soaking up the warmth while he worked at his briar pipe and surveyed the finished job of repairing the big barn. When he saw Dawson approaching, a stiffness came into the man; he waited, unspeaking, his deep-set eyes meeting the other's look coldly.

Bill Dawson read no particular meaning in this. He gave Klebold a curt nod in greeting and came directly to the point. 'It's about the wagons. You said you'd have the money this week. If you're ready to close the deal, we can make delivery whenever you say.'

The freighter did not answer for a long minute. His hollow cheeks sucked against his teeth as he pulled at the pipe-stem, built up a cloud of smoke that the stir of the warm air moved lazily. Taking the pipe from his mouth then, he said flatly, 'I've changed my mind. I ain't interested!'

'Not interested?' Bill tried to keep the hollow dismay from his voice. 'I . . . we considered it was settled.'

'There was nothin' in writing. I reckon a man has a right to change his mind. I've decided I don't need no second-hand junk. I'm putting in orders for new rolling stock and teams; so I guess it looks like we got nothing to talk about.'

He turned his back and stalked into the office. Bill Dawson was left staring, unable to fathom the reason behind this change.

There was something here, certainly — some cause he couldn't lay a finger on. It wasn't just that Tag Klebold had waked up to the fact that the hard bargain he had thought he was driving with the Trents, for those old wagons, was not such a bargain after all. If he was actually going to the extreme of stocking up with expensive new equipment, then something must have happened to encourage him in such extravagance. Tag Klebold was a cheapskate by nature, and this was utterly unlike him.

Dawson, shaking his head, had to give it up. And as he turned to leave the yard, he caught sight of the redhead, O'Shay, watching him.

O'Shay looked troubled and for an instant Bill thought he meant to speak, but then the Irishman cut a scowling glance towards the office and something seemed to decide him otherwise. He headed for the barn, instead, and Bill Dawson took his departure in a troubled mood.

He hated the necessity of telling Lila

Trent that the sale of the old stock had fallen through; but when he reached the Fair Play yard he found that she had bad news of her own. She called to him from the office doorway, and as he entered he saw at once that her face was colourless, her eyes dark with emotion.

'Slater was just here,' she told him abruptly.

Dawson felt the prickling of apprehension across his neck, along the backs of his strong hands. 'Slater — in town?'

'He stopped in for only a minute or two . . . long enough to tell me what we already knew very well; that there's no hope of any consideration from him. He's calling in his notes, as fast as they come due. He says we've acted with poor faith, and in ways that are detrimental to his interests.'

'Damn him!' Bill grunted. 'Did he say what he was going to do for freight service up to Renner?'

'He told me he was making — other arrangements.'

Dawson thought of his encounter

with Tag Klebold, and Tag's change of manner; and he wondered if he didn't have the answer. He had known it was inevitable that those two would sooner or later reach an agreement; but it had come much earlier than he expected.

He found himself wondering, too, what other reason there had been to bring Steve Slater down here, when affairs in Renner Valley were in their present perilous condition. But guesswork was futile, and he had no spare time to waste on it.

It was the redhead, O'Shay, who brought him his first real news, seeking Bill out where he sat in a booth at the eat shack having a sober meal. The Irishman slid into the seat opposite, casting a nervous look around the place to determine if he was being observed; the hour was late, however, and the room was deserted. He said, bluntly, 'I want to talk to you!'

'Looked a little that way, this morning at Klebold's.' Dawson waited, finishing the last of his coffee. There was, he figured, no reason to mistrust the redhead, or to dislike him even though he worked for Klebold. He had served the Trents loyally, for a year or more, before retrenchment forced them to lay him off.

This conflict in loyalties seemed to be bothering him now; after another moment's hesitation he said harshly, 'I ain't any turncoat. I take Klebold's pay and I wouldn't do anything to hurt the man I work for. Still, I think a lot of Lila and the old man and what's afoot now bothers me considerable.'

'Such as what? '

'Matter of fact, I ain't just sure. But there's something going on. It's Steve Slater. He was in and out of the office last night, closeted with Tag. I seen him there.'

Bill nodded slowly, at this confirmation of his own hunch. 'Slater broke off with the Trents this morning, formally; so I guessed he and Klebold must have made an arrangement.'

'Oh. Then what I'm telling you isn't news.' O'Shay lifted his thick shoulders, and moved to rise from the table. 'Well, it just seemed to me that if the Trents still were counting on help from Slater, they ought to be told the truth.'

'And thanks,' said Dawson, quickly. 'It was damned decent of you, Mike. They'll figure the same.'

O'Shay stood beside the booth, reluctant to leave. 'Just what it all adds up to, I wish I knew. Klebold pulled out not an hour ago, a special haul up to Renner Valley — a job for Slater, apparently, and something mighty urgent for him to have taken the wagon himself.'

'What's he loading?'

'That, I dunno — I wasn't around. But so far as I'm aware, we didn't have anything that was consigned for up there; and I can't locate anyone who helped get the rig ready. Looks to me like one hell of a funny business.'

Bill Dawson frowned, digesting this. It struck a false note somewhere — a warning bell that troubled him. 'Is Slater still in town?' he demanded, suddenly.

'Can't tell you that either. I know I haven't seen him.'

Without understanding just why, the other all at once knew that this was a thing that needed looking into. There were the people of South Renner, now engaged in open war with Slater. And there were the Trents, and their unscrupulous rival who had tied himself to Slater's will. This made it necessary to keep track of whatever Tag Klebold might be up to.

'Left within the hour, you said? 'And as O'Shay nodded, Dawson was already on his feet, ringing coins on the table while he reached hurriedly for his hat. He was close to a run, heading for the Trent Line stable.

16

In saddle, with the town behind him, Bill Dawson kept pushing because there was a strong lead that must be recovered. It was a fine day for riding, the sun warm but not oppressive; a winey clarity in the atmosphere made each separate spire of conifer upon the northern hills stand out with startling vividness, against the high vault of the sky. To a man's eye, distance was nothing on such a day, and the air had a special tang to it.

The chestnut bay gelding had not been on the trail in some time and it stepped out eagerly enough, so that Bill Dawson hardly needed to use the spurs at all. As the dusty wagon road he followed dipped and climbed across the foothills, working gradually upward towards the higher bulwark of the timbered wall, he kept a watch ahead for any sign of Klebold's freight rig. The marks of its wheels were plain in the road surface; and presently, topping a high and barren shoulder, Bill did in fact get a glimpse of the outfit, as it crossed a cedar-fringed meadow miles ahead of him.

He pulled in, studying it across the distance for the brief minute that it remained visible. Every detail was clear, on a tiny scale. The canvas was pulled down tightly, however, and laced close across the rear bow, and there was no way to discover or guess at what Tag Klebold's cargo might be. When the wagon and teams had disappeared again into the screen of trees beyond, Dawson shifted his attention to the land that lay ahead of him. It should not be too difficult a terrain for a mount and rider, travelling light. Quickly, with his eye, he sketched out a course that ought to save him miles and might even put him first at the Loops, and at the entrance to South Renner. Determinedly, he struck out on this new route.

As soon as he left the well-graded wagon road he got into trouble for himself and the chestnut. Even so he was saving time and he stuck to it, resting the horse frequently, and at some of the steepest climbs dropping from saddle to do the job on foot. Time dragged out, and the sun hung lower above the rugged hills to westward. The front range marched directly before him, high and towering now.

He had lost all trace of the freight outfit, but when at last he picked up the road again, at the foot of the high Loops, his quick anxious search found no evidence of tyre-sign in the dust. So he knew he had made it, though by probably a very narrow margin.

He took the switchbacks, and stepped down and gave the chestnut a rueful slap on its sweaty shoulder. 'Seems like a dirty trick to play on a horse, fellow,' he said. 'But it's something I got to do. Sorry!'

Scanning the ground, he found a stone of the size he wanted and, lifting the horse's near hind hoof, forced the pebble beneath the frog. When he set the hoof back upon the ground and, taking the reins, led the gelding for a few steps, the animal responded with a very satisfactory limp. He knew the stone would not actually hurt it, so long as Bill did not try to ride that way; and this was an emergency that called for drastic measures.

'It should do the trick,' he muttered. 'So now we start walking.'

He had led the limping bay perhaps a mile up the trail when the sound of wagon wheels and harness chains began across the utter stillness of this high upland.

Dawson stopped, turning to wait like that with the tired horse droop-headed beside him. The afternoon was far gone, now; a long, golden light lay across the rocks and brush around him, and the timber of the shouldering hill masses held already the shadows of dusk.

Then Tag Klebold brought his outfit around a turn, to find a man afoot, one hand lifted in greeting, the other holding the reins of his trail-stained mount. Half-blocking the chopped-out trail as they did, they gave the freighter little choice but to halt his teams. And the expression on Klebold's face when he recognized the other man was a plain, half comical look of startled dismay.

He made no move, and no word passed his slack lips.

'Afternoon,' called Bill Dawson, cheerfully. 'You don't know how glad I am to see somebody. My bronc pulled a ligament or something, and it looked like I'd have to hoof it all the way in to McHail's! 'As he spoke he artfully contrived for the chestnut to move a step or two, demonstrating its undeniable limp.

He waited, and still for a long moment Klebold said nothing. Then the man shifted position, and tongued his lips.

'Goin' to McHail's, you say?' His eyelids lowered, but they could not conceal the look that stabbed at Bill Dawson — a look of such pure malevolence that the latter was for a moment shaken.

He had not thought there was room for murder in Tag Klebold's small soul, but it was murder that looked at Bill Dawson just then; it made him think of the gun in his own holster, and lifted his hand to where it was only inches away from the Bisley's familiar rubber grip.

This was a very lonely spot, and isolated beyond description. If Klebold actually had it in him to kill a man, he would never choose a better place for it.

But nothing happened. Whatever might have been in the man's mind, he put it from him with a shrug of his bony shoulders. He said, sourly, 'Damned if I wouldn't enjoy to see you walk that distance!'

'Aw, now,' Bill protested, trying to keep his manner easy. 'We've had our differences but you wouldn't make a gent wear his feet off clear to the ankles? I'll just tie my bronc onto the tailgate and join you. I won't hold you up a second.'

'You stay away from — ' Klebold started in a strained shout; but he checked himself.

Bill Dawson was already moving around towards the back of the wagon, and the freighter let him go; he waited hunched on the box, giving an odd impression of one torn by divided counsels. And when Bill came back and swung lightly up to the seat beside him, Klebold yelled harshly at his teams and got the outfit rolling again up the steep trail, almost without attention for the other man.

As for Bill Dawson himself, a strange uneasiness had stirred within him as soon as he took his place next to Klebold. It wasn't fear of the man beside him: even if he had read that look aright and Tag Klebold would indeed have killed him if he dared, Bill was utterly confident of being able to hold his own. Just the same, some deep-buried fiddle-foot instinct was speaking to him, telling him that all was not well here and that he was in grave peril.

Something was wrong — something about this very wagon, with its canvas drawn tight across the bows so that his curious glance was unable to find an opening, and discover the nature of the strange cargo Tag Klebold was hauling up to Renner in such unusual haste.

He had already guessed most likely it was guns and boxes of ammunition inside the wagon, destined for the use of Big S killers against the farmers of South Renner. If he could just find out for sure, he would probably not have too much trouble taking the shipment away from Klebold.

Only, there was that nagging, troubling unease that stirred the short hairs along his neck, made him want to keep a hand on his Eisley .45's rubber handle. He wished he could explain it . . .

The team and wagon crawled around another turn in the rocky trail, and now Dawson thought he at any rate understood why Klebold had stemmed his impulse towards violence. For at the mouth of the pass which formed the southern funnel-entrance into Renner Valley, a man stood with a rifle across his folded arms. Tag Klebold must have known about this sentry, and that it wouldn't be safe to risk a shot within his hearing.

He was a farmer, in heavy farm shoes

and bib overalls and a battered straw hat; and he waited with the gun ready until the wagon was close enough for him to make out the two on the wide seat. When he recognized both to be men whom the South Renner families counted as their friends, the guard relaxed and lifted a hand in greeting.

Klebold stopped his wagon, in the shadow of the notch, and the man moved out to them.

'Keeping a guard at both ends, are you?' said Dawson. 'Not a bad idea.'

'We intend to know just who crosses our land; can't be too careful.' He looked at the wagon. 'Nothing for us, I reckon?'

'Goin' on through,' Klebold told him shortly. 'I'm tryin' to make Renner City tonight.'

'Well, then I won't hold you up — that'll take some humping!' The guard stepped back, waving them on. 'Go right ahead.'

'How are things in the valley?' Bill Dawson asked quickly.

'Quiet . . . quiet so far. Still, we figure that's only because Slater can't think of a way to get at us.'

Tag Klebold was already starting his teams, impatient to be off. There was time for one last question. 'Has he come up from below yet?'

'No.'

After that they were into the tilting notch, and the sentry was lost behind them.

And now at last they came down into the lower end of South Renner, with the patchwork of cultivated farmlands spread before them. Renner Peak's vast shadow spread far across these acres, with the sun dropping behind the ridges sawtoothed with pine and fir. A chill was in the air, off the snowfields that clung to the upcountry.

Tag Klebold asked, in a surly voice, 'You stopping the night at the McHails'?'

'I figure to,' Bill answered; and wondered at the other's curiosity. Klebold wasn't talking merely to make conversation. Dawson added, pointedly, 'I got no business pressing enough to make me try to cover all the distance to North

Renner in one day.'

This was a hint but the freighter merely grunted, not volunteering any information about his own mission. Again a silence fell between them. There was little incentive to talk above the slam and rattle of a freight wagon, the squeak of timbers and the jingle of harness-metal. You had to shout to make yourself heard distinctly.

Up the trough of the valley, paralleling the brawling stream that was full and busy now with the run-off of melting snow higher in the hills. Past the farmsteads that showed the industry which had gone into their fields.

And now the buildings of the most substantial of all these modest places came into sight — the big barn, the house of good lumber painted and well cared for, the neat flower-beds around the front porch which one day soon would be bright with the spring colours. 'McHail's,' said Bill Dawson . . . and then paused with a jerk, other words dying on his lips.

It was a different sound that he had heard, just then — something other than the monotonous medley of noises the wagon and horses churned up, and yet so nearly covered by these that he was quickly doubtful whether he had really heard it at all. It seemed to have come from behind him, from beyond the tight-drawn canvas wagon-cover . . . and it had been like the scrape of a boot heel across boards.

The uncertainty whether this might be a trick of his imagination helped to raise the quick, cold sweat that all at once sprang out upon his face, and the painful tightening of his shoulder muscles. Wondering whether Klebold had noticed anything, he shot the man a sideward look; but Klebold was scowling at the rumps of his horses, his face showing nothing readable.

But if what Bill had heard was true, it explained much: the nature of Klebold's mysterious errand — of his carefully guarded cargo and the unnamed peril Bill had sensed hanging over him, from the moment he stepped up to the seat of this wagon.

Now, however, they were almost upon the McHail place and Bill Dawson was grateful for that. He wanted mainly to get away from there. He told Tag Klebold, 'Well, I guess this is where I'll be leaving you,' and in his eagerness was already on his feet, ready to throw a leg across the side of the box without waiting for the rig to come to a stop.

Perhaps he showed himself too anxious; that, maybe, gave him away. A voice which was not Klebold's — a voice he recognized — said softly: 'I don't think you're going anywhere. Just set back, mister, like you were!'

Dawson, poised, whipped a glance across his shoulder. The tight canvas at the bow had parted; the face that showed there was the broad, fleshy face of big Steve Slater. And the metal that gleamed in Slater's hand was a six-gun, trained squarely on Bill Dawson's bent-over shape.

Bill looked at the gun, measuring the

distance and knowing the futility of thinking about his own holstered weapon. He looked squarely into Slater's muddy eyes. Slater said, again, 'You're not leavin'. This is the payoff and it's one play you're not going to spoil for me!' There was the click of his gunhammer snapping to full cock.

Then, daring its threat, Bill Dawson hurled himself sideward in a long and desperate leap.

17

He put everything into the gamble, figuring big Slater would be hesitant about
firing a shot; and his guess was right.
Slater held off the trigger just an instant
too long — long enough that the bullet drilled within an inch of Dawson's
jack-knifing figure, as he went from sight
over the edge of the wagon.

Dawson struck the turning wheel and
then the ground came up and smote him
a jolting blow, that all but pounded the
wind out of him. It sent the world spinning, but when he got to his hands and
knees, there was the freight rig, pulling
away from him. Dawson groped and
fumbled the Bisley out of his holster,
swept it up and forward and slapped a
bullet into the canvas covering.

It fetched startled shouts from within;
the hood was suddenly jerked free of
the rear bow, giving him a glimpse at
shadowy figures. Then lead sang from a

couple of guns, and one bullet struck so close it dug a gout of grit from the road-bed directly in front of his face.

Bill's chestnut gelding, terrified at the near flash of the guns, trumpeted wildly . . . gave a jerk that loosened the knot he had fastened, not too securely, in the reins. Tearing free, the gelding scampered away from there just as Bill came lunging to his feet.

Someone was running, crying out excitedly; he saw it was Tom McHail, hurrying from the farmhouse with surprising speed for one of his years, an old Sharps rifle clutched in gnarled, work-toughened hands. Between shots, Bill called warning: 'Slater and a bunch of gunmen are hidden in that rig. Klebold sneaked them in past your guard!'

Now Tag had commenced whipping up his horses, to send them into a quick burst of speed. The men inside had loosened the canvas and even as the wagon rolled away from him a regular barrage answered Dawson's firing. Nearby he heard the bellow of Tom McHail's

Sharps, throwing off a hasty shell. Bill shot the Bisley dry; by that time, the wagon and its murderous cargo were already out of range.

He had just broken his gun to shake out the empties when a muffled scream pulled him quickly towards the house.

Mrs. McHail stood in the doorway, hands cramming her apron into her mouth. And he saw then that old Tom was down, sprawled atop his smoking rifle . . . horribly still with blood staining the white of his beard. In a hurry Dawson got to him, but his legs were unsteady from fear of what he would discover.

When Mrs. McHail came running, however, he was able to tell her, 'Tom's alive. But the bullet sliced his throat and he's bleeding bad . . . '

The woman had a reserve of efficient strength, that through the years had withstood many blows and did not fail her now. She looked as white as the cloth of her spotless apron, but her voice was steady. 'Would you bring him inside, please?'

Steve Slater would have to wait. Bill gathered the hurt old man into his arms, finding him hard but almost without weight; gently he toted him in, to place him on the bed that Mrs. McHail had readied. Tom lay without movement. His eyes were closed, and there was that steady pulse of crimson flowing from the bloody crease along his deeply-seamed neck.

It seemed to Bill Dawson, though — little as he knew of surgery beyond the rough-and-ready practices of the frontier — that its flow was slackening. Mrs. McHail had returned now with clean cloths, and a basin of steaming water; he said, 'I don't think it was the jugular, ma'am. Bleeding looks like it might ease off. But since I guess there's not much I could do to help, I better be getting!'

She gave him a look. 'Slater?'

'The man's pulling a sneak play. He's got to be stopped, and that wagon full of guns.'

'What does he mean to do with them?'

'I wish I could guess! 'In the doorway

he paused long enough to add, quickly, 'I'll send help if I can.' After that he was racing from the house, thumbing new shells for his emptied six-gun as he went.

Shadows were lengthening down the deep throat of the valley; already, lights were glinting in some windows. The sun was gone and night would not be an hour distant. The gelding, calmed now, was grazing beside the road and Bill gave a whistle and ran to it . . . was almost in saddle before he remembered and, stepping down again, pulled out his knife and snapped open a blade.

It took but a moment to dig out the sliver of rock from beneath the chestnut's shoe. Inspection showed that it had done no injury; grunting satisfaction, he pocketed the knife, swung astride.

'All right, pony,' he said. 'Let's go!'

Despite the delay at McHail's, the wagon did not have too great a lead on him. He could even smell the tang of dust its broad wheels, and the hoofs of the running teams, had churned up.

He thought he should overtake them by the time they hit the drift fence.

★ ★ ★

It had been no picnic for Steve Slater, packed in with five others beneath that tight-pulled wagon cover, sun on canvas raising a broiling temperature and such a stench of sweating bodies that a man could hardly breathe. All this had ground his nerves down cruelly; and now that he saw his schemes gone suddenly awry, Slater's fury was a dreadful thing indeed.

Red of face, shirt and even the legs of his jeans dark with sweat, he clung to the wagon bow in back of Klebold and his tongue lashed the man unmercifully. 'You stupid fool! Taking him right up on the box with you! Couldn't you guess what he was after? Didn't you have brains enough to see we couldn't run that risk?'

Klebold hurled a protest across hunched shoulder: 'It would have looked funny if I turned him down!'

'I suppose you like the looks of it this

319

way?' Slater fought for balance as one of the gunmen he'd hired in Fair Play was hurled against him by the wagon's mad jolting. Cursing, he dragged a sleeve across his sweating face. 'The whole plan is shot to blazes, now. I think I dropped McHail with a bullet, but Dawson will be in saddle by this time and rousing all the rest of them ... more than we can handle!'

Klebold said, 'They won't dare follow us through the fence.'

'What makes you so sure we'll get through ourselves? The guard is bound to hold us up and even a few minutes could be fatal!'

Tag Klebold told him, 'You just lay low. I can talk our way through.'

'Maybe!' Slater's tone was bitterly sarcastic. 'You don't seem able to manage any job I've given you, yet ... ' But a moment later his big hand dropped heavily on the freighter's shoulder. 'I got an idea! Pull in, at this place just ahead of us.'

'The Burke farm? What do you want

there?'

'You'll see! Do as you're told.'

Few of the nester places were set as near the road as this one. Smoke curled from a stovepipe chimney, indicating that supper would be already on the stove. In the yard, with a clothes basket half-filled beside her, Jean Burke was taking down a washing. She had turned to stare at the fast rolling wagon, the running horses; now, as Tag Klebold reluctantly obeyed and hauled his teams to a blowing stop, she came hurrying over.

'What is it?' she cried anxiously. 'Is there anything wrong?'

Prodded, Klebold did his part — not liking it, but in the habit now of following Slater's orders. 'It's your paw, Miz Burke,' he told her, improvising feverishly. 'Tom's been shot, and the old lady needs you. If you hop in, I'll fetch you back.'

The girl had gone pale but she stood rooted, making no move to obey. Desperation turned Klebold's voice harsh and rough-edged. 'I said, hop in! You want your paw to die while you're standin' there?'

'No . . . no!' She added, 'You needn't bother, though; I'll saddle up one of our horses. Dave's on fence guard. You'll tell him, will you, what's happened?'

Before the freighter could protest, she had turned away . . . only to halt in her tracks. For Steve Slater, leaping across the tailgate, had come round the end of the wagon and intercepted her. Slater's muddy eyes held impatience and fury. 'No you don't!' he gritted. 'Get into that wagon!'

Jean Burke cried out and tried to run from him, but he was too quick. He grabbed her wrist, hauled her back with an arm-wrenching jerk. 'Listen to me!' he said tightly, his face inches from her own. 'We're going through the gate and you got to see to it that husband of yours don't try to stop us. Is that clear?'

Frightened, not understanding anything of this, Jean started fighting him. Steve Slater lifted a thick palm, brought it sharply across her face in a blow that stung and stunned; and at once she subsided. After that he was hauling her forcibly towards the wagon, where other hands reach to help drag her across the tailgate.

Swinging aboard himself, then, Slater yelled a triumphant order to Tag Klebold: 'This should do it, I figure. Start rolling . . . '

* * *

With the dropping of the sun behind western ridges, Dave Burke had begun to like his job less than ever. He had felt a growing unease throughout the long afternoon — a conviction that, after a day and more of inactivity, the conflict with Big S was due for some kind of explosion. His suspicions had been stronger since, an hour past, he caught sight of a horseman in the timber fringe over on Big S range . . . a rider who appeared to be keeping silent lookout on the fence, and the road that it chopped in two.

That rider, Dave felt, was waiting

for something — expecting something: something that boded no good for the defenders of the drift fence line. Wondering what this could be and when it would come, he saw the sun slide from view behind the pine-thick ridge and shadow flowed up across his vantage point in the rocks; and the coldness he felt was more than the chill of approaching evening. For, as soon as dusk descended and things took on the deceptive quality of half-vision, would be the time of greatest danger.

He felt this so keenly that his six-shooter was in his hand, all at once, as he heard a noise that he recognized next instant to be only the whimper of a cony somewhere in the rocks. Ruefully, he shoved the weapon back behind his waistband, and began to build a smoke to occupy his thoughts.

The shadow of the far ridge had spread clear up the wall behiud him, now, and the rocks were losing the warmth they had stored from hours of sunlight. Across the gap, Frank Harris showed himself briefly as he stood, placed both hands in the small of his back and went up on his toes, pulling cramped muscles.

Then, around a spit of land to southward, a big freight wagon showed itself, its canvas a ghostly glimmer in thickening shadows.

Tag Klebold had curbed his wild speed but as the horses came on towards the fence they were still holding to a gait that seemed somehow very odd to Dave Burke. He rose up from his place of concealmeut to call out: 'Hi, there! What's wrong?'

The freighter had pulled to a halt now; the weary horses blew and stamped with the leaders' noses all but touching the wire. Klebold, already climbing from the wagon seat, answered shortly, 'Stay put — I'll manage the gate. There's nothin' wrong.'

But Dave wasn't satisfied; some unnamed impulse decided him and started him scrambling down across the rocks, towards where Klebold was hurrying to unfasten the wide, double panels.

'Wait a minute . . . ' he began. And when Klebold paid no attention, taut nerves suddenly slipped Burke's hold on his temper. 'Damn it, I said wait! I want to talk to you!'

His sharp tone brought the other whipping around to face him. The freighter's bony skull was without colour against the dusk, as he said in a voice that didn't sound natural, 'I'm in somewhat of a hurry, boy . . . '

'I've never seen you in *this* big a hurry!' Young Burke had reached the edge of the rocks and was on level ground, still moving forward. 'What's got into you, Tag?'

Klebold's whole body twitched, uncontrollably. 'For your own damn good, boy, I warn you not to try and hold me up here!'

And then, as the young man kept walking towards the stalled wagon, a shrill and unexpected cry broke upon the stillness: 'Dave! Go *back!*'

He jerked to a halt in midstride. 'Jean!' In that instant he saw her.

She was in the forward bow of

the wagon, her arms twisted behind her — held fast in a man's strong grip. Beyond her, Dave barely glimpsed the bulky frame of Steve Slater. 'Do as I tell you, Burke!' the cattleman warned harshly. 'Stand aside — and don't touch a gun or I can't promise what might happen to your wife! We're going through this gate, do you understand?'

As Dave Burke froze, unable in his horror to do so much as lift a finger, the Big S boss added: 'Tag, what are you waiting for? Damn you — move!'

It was then that a pulse of hoofbeats, unnoticed before, suddenly imposed itself upon the awareness of them all. From the wagon sounded a startled cry: 'Watch out! *Here they come!*'

Riders were boiling up, out of the settling dusk . . . four of them, men of South Renner, with Bill Dawson in the lead. A gun within the wagon cracked sharply, even before they had got into range. A second joined it — and then the whole battery of Slater's gunmen had opened fire.

Immediately the attackers were spreading out to make poorer targets. But they didn't stop; they were shooting back as they closed in. Fear for Jean choked off the cry that swelled Dave Burke's throat. He remembered his own gun and was fumbling for it when the near winging of a bullet past him pulled his attention belatedly towards Tag Klebold.

The freighter was shooting at him, standing in a crouch with the frightened teams stirring and squealing at his back. Almost impatiently, because his whole mind was consumed in the danger to his wife, Dave flipped his gun in the man's direction and shot twice.

His first bullet missed and grazed one of the horses, sent it screaming to pile up on the others in a hopeless tangle of hoofs and harness. But the second bullet found a mark. Tag Klebold's skinny body arched backward and he dropped to his knees, throwing his gun away . . . collapsed slowly upon his side.

Dave Burke scarcely knew of it. He saw only that his wife had managed, in the confusion, to break free of Slater's hands and that she was scrambling across the wagon seat, down the big wheel to the ground. He regained his voice and called, 'This way!' and started forward as she came running through the swirling racket of the guns.

Then he saw her falling headlong. It was as though the heartbeat had ceased inside of him.

18

Bill Dawson heard his own voice shouting orders, and was halfway astonished that they made sense: 'Quit saddle! Hit the ground — a mounted man makes too good a target for guns barricaded up like that.'

He took his own advice and was leaping down, as he yelled, throwing a leg across the horn and leaving the leather in a flying hurdle. His hands were full, with the Bisley and with certain other objects which he had grabbed up, on inspiration, at Ty Rogers' barn. He tripped and went rolling; lay like that a moment while he got his breath back. Then he pushed himself up, to look around.

Rogers and the others, he saw, had also hit the dirt, letting their horses go in a crazy, gun-shy scatter. He didn't think any of his men had collected a bullet in that first wild charge; he himself had a painful furrow that a slug had raked along the side of his left forearm but he could give it little attention.

In some astonishment he had watched that girl clambering out of the wagon, not even knowing who it was until he heard Dave Burke's agonized cry, as she suddenly and alarmingly fell. With deep, nearly painful relief, he had seen Dave rush to her and help her up to her feet again. Quickly caught breath eased from him as he realized she must only have lost her footing for an instant . . . now Dave had managed to get his wife into the talus heapings and there she would be safe enough.

Guns were rattling steadily, all along on that narrow gap.

Bill Dawson raised to one knee and emptied a couple of shells himself, aiming at the flash of six-shooters forted up within the stalled freight rig. But he knew the stout construction of those ancient wagons of Klebold's: built for tough mountain travel, they were thoroughly capable of turning aside six-gun bullets, as long as Slater and his hired guns kept low. And meanwhile, dusk was settling with the rapidity of a mountain twilight.

Come night they would likely be able to quit the wagon, slip through the fence and escape. The farmers knew this, but there seemed no way they could settle this thing before daylight failed them utterly.

For that reason Bill Dawson figured it was a lucky break that, when he picked the four of them up at Ty Rogers' place, he'd also had the impulse to stop and grab up certain odds and ends of material on a hunch that they would serve him now. And so he stabbed his six-gun into holster and went to work, knowing this was the only hope.

He had an axe handle, and an old barn lantern that was reassuringly full of liquid. For the rest, the shirt off his own back would do. Quickly he stripped out of it, knotted its sleeves to one end of the wood. The rank odour of kerosene bit into his nostrils as he emptied the lantern's contents onto the shirt, soaking it freely. With the improvised torch ready, he lurched to his feet.

He would have to get in closer. He hurried forward at a crouch, right into gunfire; but the dusk was so thick by this time that he knew he made a poor target. Near enough, he knelt again . . . hastily thumbed alive the match he held, ready.

The tiny flame spurted up, flickered. Then, as he dropped it into the folds of the shirt, the kerosene took fire with a great whoosh of sound. And, springing up, Bill Dawson swung his torch in a circle about his half-naked body; let it go, to describe a bright arc and drop full upon the canvas cover of Tag Klebold's wagon.

For an instant the impact seemed to have smothered out the flames . . . then they leaped higher again and all at once that ancient canvas went up with a roar. A consuming fury of fire swept the wagon, from front to tail. The bows stood forth briefly, darkly, like a skeleton's ribs. Then they, too, had caught and became bright, flaming arches; while, with frenzied cries, Slater's gunmen were scrambling out of the freight rig that had all at once become a trap.

After that, of course, the rest was easy.

Bill Dawson held his gun, waiting for one particular target while he let the men behind him take care of these other, black silhouettes. Almost in a matter of seconds, it seemed, the fight was broken, the last of the crew throwing up his hands and loudly offering surrender. Yet Bill had still not located the one he'd marked for his own.

He wondered if Steve Slater were already dead, in that burning wagon, or under the hoofs of the wildly tangled and frightened horses. He was about to move in cautiously, hunting for him, when he heard Frank Harris's wild shout, down from the rocks:

'Watch it! Watch it! Here's Big S — !'

And here indeed they were, hurling themselves out of the night and against the fence . . . come to help their boss who was in trouble. It was a good deal like suicide; but these were brave men who rode for Slater, whatever else might have been said of them. And suddenly Dawson sighted the gross shape of one who stood in stirrups and yelled hoarsely at the rest.

Before he could fire, Virg Noonan had lost himself again in the tangle of horsemen. Bill ran forward, straight up to the fence. There was Noonan — holding his panicked horse steady while he reached with smoking gunmuzzle to try and flip the catch that held the big double gate closed. He saw Bill and, still leaning from saddle, swivelled his gun and flung a shot at him between the wires.

Dawson fired at the same instant, and both bullets hit. Lead took Noonan squarely, toppled him from his slant-wise perch in the saddle, thudded him lifeless into the hoof chopped dirt. But at the same moment, the terrific impact that struck Bill Dawson's hip spilled him and sent him rolling. He lost his gun. Somehow he got to hands and knees, searching blindly for it . . . and heard the voice that lifted his head, dazedly, towards the burning wagon.

Bloody, his skin fire-blackened and clothes smouldering, Steve Slater stood there not a dozen feet away. The Big S boss had himself propped crazily upon an injured leg, and one arm in a bloody sleeve dangled uselessly. But the other hand held a sixshooter, levelled.

'You done it to me, Dawson!' he cried hoarsely. 'You ruined me! But at least, I'll get you!'

There didn't seem to be any strength left in Bill. He could only crouch and look at that hatred, and at the tunnel-like revolver muzzle. He saw Slater's face work spasmodically, saw the gun level for certain aim.

Then the gun began to wobble, insanely, and the bloody face suddenly broke in agony. The strength Slater had hoarded for this last effort just was not enough. His fingers let the gun drop and slowly, ponderously, he toppled forward upon it.

Bill passed out, himself, then.

★   ★   ★

He lay in the spare bedroom at the McHail place, looking through the window at banners of golden light that rested upon the pine ridges; and as memory of the fight crowded into his mind he thought that this brightness in the sky was the fitting symbol of a dawn that would be breaking now over Renner Valley, with Slater and Noonan dead, and the power of Big S broken.

But as the colours faded he realized it was not sunrise he was watching, but the last ebbing of the day. He must have slept the clock around, for he had no knowledge of anything since blacking out. Perhaps, even, it was more than one day he had lain here . . . Alarmed, he tried to roll over in the bed and found that one of his legs was stiff and beyond feeling, and that his left arm was heavily bandaged.

Then, a hand was placed upon his shoulder and Lila Trent's voice said quickly, 'Not too fast, now! You lost a lot of blood.'

Bill craned his neck and looked at

her, in astonishment. She seemed pale in the growing dusk of the room, and tired-looking. She sat in a chair beside the bed and he blurted, 'Where did you come from?'

'I rode up with the doctor,' she said. 'When word came, down at Fair Play, I thought perhaps I could help. We got here just a little while ago . . . '

The sound of talking had brought someone in from the kitchen of the house. It was Dave Burke, standing in the doorway and grinning at Bill. 'Woke up, did you? We figured you needed all the rest you could get! That bullet in your leg nicked an artery, and you'd drained plenty before we could get you patched together. But the doc says you should be all right in a few weeks.'

Bill Dawson said, disgustedly, 'Don't know why I couldn't have stuck it out to the end of the act!'

'It's all taken care of. Tag Klebold died this morning, but he talked a lot, at the end. He told us of Steve Slater's scheme, with that wagon load of gunmen. They'd meant to overpower the gate guard, throw it open for Virg Noonan to run a stampede of beef through and wipe us out. You out-smarted them all, Bill — and Noonan and the crew destroyed themselves trying to save Slater from his own trap!'

Dawson heard this in sober silence. Then, looking past Dave into the empty kitchen, he asked, 'The McHails — and the rest? Did we — make out too badly?'

'Why, Tom is resting now; he'll recover, though at his age it'll take him somewhat longer than, say, for a young buck like you. No one else was even badly hit. We came through light — awfully light.'

'Sure glad to hear it! What about Jean?'

'Not hurt at all. But I think I could have killed Slater, with my two bare hands . . .'

Then Lila Trent said, smiling, 'It's all over now. There are things about it we'll want to try and forget. But it shouldn't be too hard . . . not when you figure everything that lies ahead!'

'For you and Jabez, too,' agreed Bill

Dawson, realizing it was so. 'With Slater and Klebold both gone, and your dad able for once to stop worrying and concentrate on getting well again I guess that whittles your problems down to a size that you can solve, in time.'

She said quickly, 'With your help, Bill!' Her eyes held a real warmth, then, that emboldened him to reach and touch the hand she laid upon his shoulder.

And Dave Burke, grinning even wider, quietly faded back through the door into the kitchen. He hadn't been an old married man too long to know the signs, when a couple of young people would rather they were left alone . . .

Other titles in the
Linford Western Library:

THE LAWLESS BORDER

Allan Vaughan Elston

It was just one year ago that the O'Hara brothers planned to buy themselves a ranch, settle down, and raise some stock. But that was before Milton disappeared the night after he won forty-four hundred dollars at a poker game. Certain that his brother was hijacked and murdered for his winnings, Lynn vows to investigate. When he arrives in Tucson, there's one man left on his list . . . and he finds himself face-to-face with the ugly muzzle of a six-gun!

BORDERS TO CROSS

Parker Bonner

It's clear that Dan Mason had a hand in killing his cousin Bill in order to gain control of the family ranch, the Lazy M. Still, Cal Holland is determined to steer clear of of another man's fight — until the fight is brought to his doorstep. Mason sends a hired killer after him. And if this wasn't already enough to stir him to action, Cal discovers that the life of Bill's sister Nancy is also threatened by Dan's ambitious greed . . .

THE HOUSE OF GOLD

Max Brand

In this trio of tales, honest thief James Geraldi embarks upon some of his greatest adventures, including a quest for the elusive Golden Horus, a gold statue inlaid with four perfect emeralds and a large, flawless yellow diamond. Whether he's seeking a treasure, protecting an innocent girl, or handling other thieves who may not be quite so honest, Geraldi remains a classic and unforgettable figure of the West.

DEATH'S TALLY

Bradford Scott

Oil and bullets — Sanderson City has swallowed plenty of both. When Walt Slade arrives to put a lid on the violence, the town is set to blow sky-high in his face. A lit fuse, a shotgun blast in the dark . . . and the ace undercover Texas Ranger is plunged into a searing sixgun showdown with a greed-crazed pack of killers.

MATCH RACE

Fred Grove

Quarter horse racing presents a thrill few men in the Old West can resist. Dude McQuinn, Coyote Walking, and Billy Lockhart are no exception, riding from town to town, matching and trading racehorses. Dude is the straight-talking front man, Coyote the jockey, and Billy the doctor, concocting potions that can cure a horse of anything — at least temporarily. But Billy is being watched by a strange man in a black bowler hat — a man who knows a secret about his past . . .